GWENDOLINE BUTLER

Gwendoline Butler is a Londoner, born in a part of South London for which she still has a tremendous affection. She was educated at Haberdashers and then read history at Oxford. After a short period doing research and teaching, she married the late Dr Lionel Butler, Principal of Royal Holloway College. She has one daughter.

Gwendoline Butler's crime novels are very popular in Britain and the States, and her many awards include the Crime Writers' Association's Silver Dagger.

She spends her time travelling, looking at pictures, and, of course, writing.

D0963600

GWENDOLINE BUTLER

A COLD COFFIN

HarperCollins*Publishers*

This novel is entirely a work of fiction. The names, characters and
incidents portrayed in it are the work of the author's imagination.
Any resemblance to actual persons, living or dead, events or
localities is entirely coincidental.

HarperCollins*Publishers*
77–85 Fulham Palace Road,
Hammersmith, London W6 8JB

The HarperCollins website address is:
www.fireandwater.com

This paperback edition 2001

1 3 5 7 9 8 6 4 2

First published in Great Britain by
Collins Crime in 2000

Copyright © Gwendoline Butler 2000

Gwendoline Butler asserts the moral right to
be identified as the author of this work

ISBN 0 00 710644 0

Set in Meridien and Bodoni

Printed and bound in Great Britain by
Clays Ltd, St Ives plc

AUTHOR'S NOTE

One evening in April 1988, I sat in Toynbee Hall in the East End of London, near to Docklands, listening to Doctor David Owen (now Lord Owen) give that year's Barnett Memorial Lecture. In it, he suggested the creation of a Second City of London, to be spun off from the first, to aid the economic and social regeneration of the Docklands.

The idea fascinated me and I have made use of it to create a world for detective John Coffin, to whom I gave the tricky task of keeping there the Queen's Peace.

A brief Calendar of the life and career of John Coffin,
Chief Commander of the Second City of London Police.

John Coffin is a Londoner by birth, his father is unknown and his mother was a difficult lady of many careers and different lives who abandoned him in infancy to be looked after by a woman who may have been a relative of his father and who seems to have acted as his mother's dresser when she was on the stage. He kept in touch with this lady, whom he called Mother, lodged with her in his early career and looked after her until she died.

After serving briefly in the army, he joined the Metropolitan Police, soon transferring to the plain-clothes branch as a detective.

He became a sergeant and was very quickly promoted to inspector a year later. Ten years later, he was a superintendent and then chief superintendent.

There was a bad patch in his career about which he is reluctant to talk. His difficult family background has complicated his life and possibly accounts for an unhappy period when, as he admits, his career went down a black hole. His first marriage split apart at this time and his only child died.

From this dark period he was resurrected by a spell in a secret, dangerous undercover operation about which even now not much is known. But the esteem he won then was recognized when the Second City of London was being formed and he became Chief Commander of its Police Force. He has married again, an old love, Stella Pinero, who is herself a very successful actress. He has also discovered two siblings, a much younger sister and brother.

1

_____

*Tuesday. One day it will be Christmas, but not
for many of those living now.*

CI Phoebe Astley spoke in a sober voice to the Chief Commander. 'I hate a headless baby,' she said. 'Terrible thought.'

Because the Chief Commander was an old friend, she felt free to drop in on Coffin with anything that worried her. So much so that Coffin had told his wife that his heart sank when Phoebe appeared in his room.

'I hate a headless anyone,' said Coffin gloomily. Not so long ago an ill-wisher had left the head of a cat on the staircase in his home in St Luke's Tower. Not something you forgot.

He looked round his office without pleasure. Stella, his wife, had told him that his chosen decorative style was ugly and he had replied that it was workmanlike, but observing it now he could see what she meant. Everything that could be dark brown was dark brown, and the rest was cream. Or, in the case of the curtains, dark blue.

'Bile,' he murmured to himself. 'That's what this room is like. I must have been bilious when I chose the colours . . . I'd probably had a row with Stella.' They used to quarrel a lot in those days, and they didn't seem to now. Was this a good sign, as he hoped? Or a bad one?

He loved her, though, he knew that, and he knew now that she loved him too. Once he had doubted, but no longer.

Phoebe went to look out the window. It was still raining, as it had been for days. The rain, washing away the light top

1

surface of soil of a recent excavation, had played its part in uncovering the head. Heads rather.

Phoebe was a tall, elegantly built woman, with a taste for dark trousers and bright sweaters. Today she was in red and black. 'There is this pit, about ten infants' skulls.' She shook her head. 'More maybe.'

'Seems enough.'

'A small population. Probably not more than five breeding pairs in the group.' This was the way students of primitive man talked about populations they were investigating. She had picked this up from one of the archaeologists working on the site. 'They couldn't feed too many children.'

'Makes me feel like King Herod.'

'No need to take it personally,' said Phoebe briskly, turning away from the window. 'Dr Murray . . . she's the archaeologist, said they are Neanderthal . . . been there for many thousands of years.'

'Some sort of a cult?' enquired Coffin.

'More like a culling . . . Dr Murray said the Neanderthals, to which, from the skulls, these children may have belonged, practised infanticide to keep the population down.' Dr Murray had not yet passed on her belief that one, and only one, of the skulls was not so old, modern-day in fact, and might have been deposited there by someone who had discovered the heads and thought this was a good place to hide another one. She always thought in terms of crimes. She would be telling John Coffin her suspicions, which might mean something or nothing; it was going to be hard to date this later skull.

The big teaching hospital that was attached to Second City University had a collection of skulls in a medical museum that was now hardly used. It was a macabre, dead place these days, but it had its uses.

'I'm hating this more and more . . . to think I've been sitting on top of them all these years.' Coffin was gloomy.

'Not exactly sitting, sir.'

He went to the window to join her. 'Well, walking, walking towards my car.'

The whole area to the north of his window, once bare, unpaved ground where a few bushes struggled for life, was being cleared. Headquarters of the Second City Police was being expanded: they had outgrown their accommodation and another new block was being put up.

Or would be put up once the ground was cleared. At the moment it was a hole. And one full of water since it was raining hard. This water-logged hole was now roped off and marked with signs saying that Entry was Forbidden.

The archaeologists had taken over, but even they had not been able to work for some days.

'Dr Murray is very excited about it. No one knew there was a concentration of Neanderthals here.'

'Still got some,' said Coffin sourly. He had come from a short working trip up north to find he had yet another problem. Neanderthals! Sometimes he felt he worked with a bunch of them. 'There's Nean Street just round the corner. Probably built on a settlement of them.' And it was true that the local kids called some of the families there – short, stocky but powerful, men and women both – Neanderthals.

'Oh no,' said Phoebe seriously. 'They died out millennia ago.'

'Think so?' said the sceptic.

He felt that he could hear the millennia marching with heavy feet, but not taking all the Neanderthals with them.

Phoebe ignored her boss's mood, partly because she always did and partly because she knew the reason for it. There was a possible murder case in the Second City that was troubling him. Troubling a lot of them, since it involved a police officer, a detective in Spinnergate. It was just possible that Arthur Lumsden had murdered his wife.

That was, if she was dead. At the moment she was just 'missing'.

He had not reported her missing, even after seven days of absence and silence. Her mother had telephoned his sergeant in the Amen Street Divisional Office.

But there was blood of her type in the family car, and talk

of a quarrel. The family dog, a small terrier, was missing too. There was a strong feeling that Lumsden might have killed his wife . . . husbands could do anything, but he would never have killed his dog.

DC Lumsden was on leave. He had given a statement, denying a quarrel but admitting they had been having a 'difficult time'. They had breakfasted together, and he had then gone on duty. When he came home there was no wife and no dog. He didn't know anything about the blood in the car. And yes, he had had a rest period of two hours in the middle of the day. No, he had not gone home, just gone for a walk.

As a statement, there were holes in it.

And there the matter rested for the time being. One of the Spinnergate CID team was looking into Mrs Lumsden's disappearance as quietly as possible. Coffin looked at the file: Sergeant Drury was the man.

Coffin knew Lumsden slightly and was now repressing the feeling that he hadn't liked the man. 'Not a joke in him.'

And then there were the murders in Minden Street. Gunshot wounds to the head. Nasty. Yes, Coffin had plenty to worry about. Phoebe was worried about them herself.

Coffin looked thinner, a trifle haggard, which she admitted to finding attractive. She always had found him attractive, but now working with him made this forbidden territory. Anyway, he had a very lovely wife, Stella Pinero, a powerful lady in her own right.

'The Neanderthal population was probably small, she says, and co-existed with modern man.'

'I just said so.'

Phoebe ignored this. She sipped the coffee that Coffin had politely offered her. He was good in that kind of way.

'Are they still underneath all that water?'

'Yes, but they are due to be carefully removed tomorrow morning, and taken off to be examined in a lab somewhere.'

Coffin felt better. 'Right, well, let's get back to what we

were discussing.' He knew what it was. Phoebe had come in several times already to talk about the same issue. 'The murders in Minden Street . . . you believe you know the murderer, but the lawyers won't let you charge him.' Interesting case, he mused. Someone ought to write it up one day, perhaps I'll do it myself.

'I thought you liked him yourself,' said Coffin cautiously. He had heard rumours.

'We knew each other for a bit. It was when I first came to the Second City and was finding my feet, thought he might make a good contact,' said Phoebe defensively. 'I hadn't got him sussed out.' She shrugged. 'So I made a mistake.'

'So what can I do?'

'He's dangerous,' went on Phoebe, as if she wasn't listening. 'He'll do it again. Bound to.'

Better wait till he 'does it again' before I embark on the book, thought Coffin.

'He says he knew you.'

'I believe we have met,' said Coffin cautiously. 'Black Jack? Yes, he is a villain . . . never thought of him as a killer, though.'

Black Jack Jackson, which was his nickname and nothing to do with any American band leader, was up for any fraud and money-making enterprise that came his way. Son and brother to the victims. Murder in the family, all right. But although a suspect – there had been a quarrel and some violence from him – any proof was hard to find.

Coffin was riffling through the papers in the file. 'Hard man to convict.'

At the suggestion that the lawyers might be right, Phoebe drew in a deep breath, so deep that Coffin thought she might blow up like an aggrieved toad and become twice her size.

'There are three dead women in that house, and if he didn't kill them, then I don't know who did.' She amplified this statement. 'It looks as though whoever did it was either let in, or had a key . . . Mrs Jackson had fitted the flat up with one of those special keys.' She repeated, 'If he didn't do it, then who did?'

'Maybe that's the answer,' suggested Coffin. 'We don't know who did it.' He shook his head.

'If you don't mind me saying so, sir, you are standing aside from this case.'

Coffin knew he was. 'The two young women . . . the sisters were . . . are' – how do you talk about the so recently dead . . . he settled for what seemed easier – 'they are friends of Stella.'

He waited a bit, then said, 'Black Jack? As killer? Not how I see him.'

'He's a friend, is he?' Phoebe pretended to be surprised, but she was never surprised who rated as a friend of the Chief Commander. He trawled in dark waters when it suited him.

'My friend? Black Jack is interested in and collects rare pornography, books, videos and manuals, all aspects: sadism, masochism, pederasty, bestialism, and he may well practise any of these that he can manage. I would be pleased to put him away for any of them if I got the chance. So, no, not a friend, nor a companion in bondage.'

'Sorry.'

'But I don't think he's a killer.'

Black Jack, his full name John Jackson, had come by his nickname because of his crop of dark curls and deep brown eyes. Also because he was a known criminal, not particularly violent, preferring to rely on cunning, which he had in abundance. He had the good sense to commit most of his crimes outside the Second City, which meant that Coffin's investigators had only been after him twice, getting him inside once. 'No hard feelings,' he had said to Coffin. 'You do your job, I do mine.' And he had offered Coffin the run of his pornographic library.

Offer refused.

Unmarried, he had lived for a while with his mother and twin sisters in Madras House in Minden Street, moving out not long before the murders.

It was these three women who had been murdered. Shot.

'I never knew Mrs Jackson, although she claimed to have known my mother.' He had found this hard to believe, his long disappeared mother being a mythical figure by now to the son she had left behind before embarking on other marriages, other lives. 'But the twins, Amy and Alice, were friends of Stella. They had worked together once. They were completely different from their brother, straight as a die Stella always said. And yet they loved him. It was their house, you know.'

'He gave it to them,' said Phoebe. She had had to admit to his generosity with his no doubt ill-gotten gains. He had offered her diamond stud earrings, which, thank God, she had refused, although her ears had ached for them, delicious glittery little objects that they were.

Coffin was silent. What do you know of people, after all?

Because of his position, which carried its own burden of responsibilities and worries, he had kept his distance from the Jackson household, although he knew that Stella enjoyed the company of the twins. He had always been too tactful to ask her what she thought of Black Jack.

'So where is he now?'

Phoebe shrugged. 'He can't go back to the house in Minden Street. It's a scene of the crime and still has forensics crawling all over it.'

This case was being handled by one of the Headquarters CID teams of which Phoebe Astley was a very active part. She was also handling one other case, that of a suspected abduction and rape, although it was coming to a successful conclusion.

'Inspector Lavender is working with me.'

Coffin nodded. 'Know him, of course.' Larry Lavender, about whose name no one dared make jokes about sexual ambivalence, was a tough operator and came from a famous political family.

'He's got ideas, not all of which I agree with.'

Larry Lavender, yes, Coffin knew him as a man of ideas. He had helped his rapid promotion.

'He says someone just walked in off the street and did it.'

'Motive?'

'He says first find the killer, and then you'll find the motive.'

'He could be right. So he doesn't think it's Jack Jackson.'

Phoebe shrugged. 'I think he'd accept that it could be Jack. Whom we can't find by the way. Never home.'

'Are you looking?'

'Not hard.'

Coffin nodded. 'Well, I won't weep for him. A man like Jack will have always a bolt hole. So where does he live . . . when he's there?'

'He used to live in the house in Minden Street. Not large, but smart. We're coming up in the world in Spinnergate, you know. Then he bought a place in Watermen's Row, near the river.'

Coffin nodded again. He did know. 'Mimsie Marker will make a meal of it.'

Mimsie kept a newspaper and flower stall by the station; she was reputed to know all the gossip of the Second City and to pass it on with expertise, adding a little gloss where she thought necessary. She was also known to be a shrewd lady with a penny, acquiring substantial investments. The story had it that she walked round the corner in her shabby working clothes and then stepped into a Roller to get home. Coffin knew this was not true: it was one of the smaller Bentleys.

When Phoebe, still muttering crossly, had gone, Coffin got back to work on the papers on his desk. He had recently initiated a study of all the clubs in his bailiwick, some of which he suspected of being involved in drug offences and allied crimes. He thumbed through the report: the Cat Lovers' Club sounded harmless enough, as did Tortoise Friends, but the Ladies of Leisure might need looking into. Several walking and hiking clubs – surely not much trouble there? But he knew from experience you could never be sure. Some were more sinister than others.

Then he put on a raincoat to go down to look at the flooded excavations.

The rain had stopped, but it was a damp, dark evening.

He looked down into the murk and wondered about the babies' heads, once buried there, now uncovered. Although dark, the water was not quite opaque; reflections shimmered and moved in the lights from the building behind. You could imagine you saw shapes.

'You could almost imagine that was a skull.' He must have spoken aloud.

'It is a skull.'

He felt a presence behind him and looked up. There was a tall, sturdily built woman in a raincoat but no hat. Her hair was wet, but she didn't seem to mind. She was attractive, he found. Coffin moved forward, as if he would try to get the skull out. In fact he wanted to; he disliked intensely the thought of an infant head resting in the mud. He crouched down, trying to get at it.

The woman put her hand on his shoulder. 'No, leave it. Let the archaeologists do it. Everything has to be mapped in situ.'

He stood up; they were about as tall as each other. 'Dr Murray, I presume?'

She nodded. 'And I know who you are, too. I know your wife.'

'You know Stella?'

'She came to a lecture I gave. Introduced herself.' Dr Murray smiled. 'You don't forget Stella once you've met her.'

'No. You're in charge here?' It was more of a statement than a question.

'I am head of the prehistory and archaeology department at the Second City University. When I got wind of the discovery here, I asked to be involved and they kindly allowed me.'

No one else wanted to do it was Coffin's cynical interpretation of this statement.

'But I'm not in charge. A whole team of archaeologists will be doing the real work.'

And then Coffin got round to what really worried him. 'I thought you were going to get all the skulls out. Still here, though.'

'That'll happen. All this rain,' she said briefly. 'Water drained in. We thought we would do more damage by rushing. It'll drain naturally quite soon.' She smiled. 'I would be chary of using the phrase "in charge" anyway. Controlling a gang of scholars and technicians is never easy: they argue.'

'I believe you.' He stared down. Was he imagining a pinkiness down there by one of the skulls? He pointed. 'Looks different.' Pinkiness. Just the light reflection. Not blood. Couldn't be blood. He had had blood on his mind since the Minden Street murders.

'This one is not Neanderthal.'

He was surprised at her certainty. 'How can you tell?'

'By the shape. It is much much later. Modern.'

He wondered what modern meant. 'How much later?'

'At the moment I cannot be sure.'

In a car at the kerb, at the wheel, was a young woman, bright blue eyes, a froth of curly fair hair and a broad smile. She was looking at them both with good-humoured amusement. 'Had enough?'

Dr Murray ignored this and introduced them. 'This is Natasha, she drives for me. Well, some of the time. Chief Commander John Coffin, Natasha Broad.'

Natasha held out a hand. 'I'm her cousin, but she doesn't like to admit it. She can't keep away from this site, can you, Mags? Fascinated by the infant skulls.'

'They are interesting,' said Dr Murray soberly. She looked at Coffin. 'You're interested yourself.'

'Of course, I am,' observed Coffin mildly. 'Were the children sacrificed, or did they die naturally?'

'I can't answer that,' said Dr Murray. 'Not at the moment, perhaps never. If I had to make a guess, then I'd say they were sacrificed.'

Coffin looked thoughtful.

'They probably ate the flesh,' observed Dr Murray. 'Neanderthals appear to have been healthy stock, but hungry. Neanderthal man ate what flesh he could get. We have found teeth marks on human bones.'

'The Neanderthals died out, though, didn't they?' said Coffin. 'To be replaced by modern man. Perhaps there weren't enough babies for them to eat. Or perhaps modern man ate the Neanderthals.'

'Possibly.'

Natasha laughed. 'Come on, let's get home.'

So they lived together, Coffin thought. Wrongly as it happened. Wonder if it's a happy household.

'Let me know about the later skull. I'm interested.'

'It's been there some time. Not a police job.'

Well, you never know, thought Coffin. 'I'm not looking for work,' he said.

Although he disliked the thought of the dead Neanderthal babies, he found himself even more troubled by the later skull. How did it get there? And why? And who put it there?

He felt a gust of fury at the thought.

'I don't think he liked what you said about the date of that one skull,' said Natasha to her cousin, who was recounting her interview with Coffin in detail as they drove to Spinnergate, where Dr Murray owned a charming late eighteenth-century house that she had restored and renovated.

Margaret Murray did not respond to this gambit. 'Odd to think that this was once one of the first homes of the English textile industry,' she said.

'Eh?'

'Spinnergate,' obliged Dr Murray. 'Weaver or webster, creating fabrics.'

'Oh you're always back in the past.' She drove on deftly. 'Now, the Chief Commander is not interested in the past.' She added thoughtfully, 'He likes a good murder.'

'Only professionally.'

'Well, he's got quite a choice at the moment.' The papers had been full of the Minden Street murders, the death of the Jackson family. Horrible, she had thought.

They drove on with Natasha humming under her breath. Sounded dirge-like. To her cousin, she looked too thin and badly dressed. Margaret didn't mind that both Nat and her husband only ever wore jeans, but you ought to wear them with style.

'Don't know what's the matter with you two. You both work all hours, but you never seem to have any money to spend.'

'Saving,' said Natasha. 'You know Jason doesn't earn much, teachers never do. And we are trying to make improvements to the house.'

'I thought Sam was helping you there.' Sam was a kind of universal slave labourer. Sam was thought by some to be simple, but closer observers like Coffin saw he had a darker side. Certainly he took a keen interest in his medical specimens. 'I might have been a doctor with a bit more luck. I reckon I'd have made a surgeon.'

'Even Sam has to be paid.'

'I shall have to take you in hand.' And she meant it.

'Don't even try.' And Natty meant it too.

'We'd better hurry to get home,' said Margaret Murray. 'Dave might be there by now.'

Dave was her husband, a stylist and cutter and Mayfair hairdresser, always on the wing to Los Angeles and New York, the winner of many prizes and medals. She was a little afraid of him, he was such a dab hand with the scissors. Like a surgeon, lovely manners, but you always remembered the knife.

'Oh, don't worry about him.' Natasha accelerated away. 'He's harmless.'

Margaret bridled a little. No one likes to believe that the

husband they have loved, bedded and married was harmless. Besides, she was not sure if it was true.

'He's not quite what he seems,' she said carefully.

'No one is quite what they seem,' said Natasha. She believed this. She got out of the car to help Margaret with her boxes and books, and limped to the door. It was a bad limping day; some days were worse than others. It was tiresome when her leg was bad. She had been a dancer once. Almost everyone has several lives, and that had been one of hers. Her very own. Others she had shared.

Margaret looked at her with a frown.

'I'll put the car round the corner. I saw a space,' said Natasha. There was no garage nor space for one; motor cars had not been envisaged when this house was built. You owned a horse, and possibly a carriage, or walked.

While Natasha parked the car, Margaret ran into the house. 'Dave?'

He was not there.

'Damn you, I'll kill you,' she said aloud just as Natasha walked in.

'Parked the car. Got the last gap, cars are terrible round here. Who are you going to kill? No, don't tell me, I can guess, he has two legs and lovely hair.'

'He said he'd be here. He promised – we were going out to dinner. It's our anniversary.'

'Your wedding?'

'No, when we met.'

'I should think you'd go into mourning for that.' Natasha went into the kitchen. 'He's been here. I can smell him. That aftershave . . . Not here now, though, probably out killing someone. You know, he does a lovely scissor cut.'

She found Dave attractive herself, but would never betray Margaret with him, in spite of temptation. There were other ways of working out frustration, as she suspected Dave knew.

'Oh, you get back to your own husband,' snapped Margaret.

'And you go looking for yours.'

She found herself thinking: Don't get into trouble, Margaret.

13

She could hear herself saying to her husband that she was worried about Margaret.

Coffin went home to Stella to tell her the story of the skulls.

'Yes, nasty, but it's a long while ago.'

'I'm not sure how much that ought to count,' said Coffin thoughtfully.

Stella did not answer. She knew he was still grieving for the death of his young assistant, DI Charlie Young, the son, the only son at that, of the Chief Superintendent with whom Coffin had worked for years. Worked gratefully, because Archie Young was hard-working and efficient. And a good man; you could trust his integrity. Archie Young had recently moved to become Chief Constable of Filham in Essex, just north of the Second City.

Charlie had died while dealing with an armed robbery in Spinnergate. He had taken a shot right in the face and never came round. His wife, Sally, was also a policewoman, a CID officer. They had recently found out she was expecting their first child. Not a good time to lose your husband.

Stella too had liked Charlie. She looked with sympathy at her husband, but decided that silence was best.

The room they were using in the tower where they lived, the oldest part of the former St Luke's Church, was a beautiful, calm place. Usually it worked its magic on Coffin, but tonight it was not doing the job. Stella believed that Coffin was quite unconscious of how the room affected him in this way: he thought he had no aesthetic sensibilities. 'Blue's blue and yellow's yellow. How could they make a difference?' She answered that it was a good job he wasn't a surgeon; he'd know the difference between red blood and no blood. Not the right thing to say to a copper – he'd seen plenty of blood in his time. She gave him an affectionate smile. She was softer on him these days.

'And then there is the later skull in there with them. Dr Murray says that it is many hundred years old, but I am not so sure.'

'Oh, she'd know.'

'Would she? Yes, if she'd examined it carefully, but as far as I know she hasn't done that yet: just had a look.'

'You've got enough to worry about, love, as well as dwelling on the dead of hundreds of years ago.'

'I don't think that skull is so old. It worries me. I want to find out more.'

'No one is in a better position than you to do so.'

He nodded. He felt better already. 'I'll set Phoebe Astley on it. She'll sort it out if anyone can.'

This was true. Phoebe was like a terrier searching for a rat when she started into anything.

'If this skull is recent, modern in fact, yet placed there with the other skulls, then someone must have known the Neanderthals were there already.'

'Yes, I've thought of that. It's a puzzle. The site was being prepared for our new building when one of the workmen, just a lad, caught a sight of the top of the pit, a layer of stones and earth. It looked different to him, clever lad, and he told the foreman. The foreman took advice and got the area cleared. Work was stopped when they saw what they'd got, it's still stopped. The archaeologists have taken photographs.'

'Observant, that workman.'

Coffin nodded. 'Turned out he was a student earning a bit of money. And interested in the past. He got more than he expected. But he says he isn't going to waste it . . . going to write it up.' He poured himself a drink. 'I had a talk with the lad himself, asked to see him.' He turned to his wife. 'Says he knows you.'

'No! What's his name?'

'Eddy Buck.'

Stella raised her eyebrows. 'Yes, I know him . . . Or I know his mother, she works in our wardrobe. She's clever too. He's done some holiday work there too. I believe he can't make up his mind whether to be a doctor or an actor.'

He could tell she liked him. Well, he was a good-looking, taking lad.

Stella studied her husband's face. He looked tired. 'You miss Archie Young.'

Archie had been gone about six months.

Coffin smiled. 'I'm glad he got the promotion he deserved. I wanted him to have it.'

'Nice man,' said Stella reflectively. 'Tough, though.'

'We had to be,' said Coffin.

'I know that. I was alive then, too, remember.'

'And I don't know that times have changed, either. May have got worse.' He looked towards Stella. 'I might need your help through this, Stella. You will help me, won't you?'

She nodded. 'It's the child, isn't it?'

Coffin nodded. 'All the children, but that later one especially.' He stood up. 'Something terrible lies behind that head, and it didn't happen thousands of years ago, either.'

'That's just a guess.'

'I'm a good guesser. It comes with experience.'

Stella watched him carefully for a moment. 'Dearest . . .'

Coffin stirred. She wasn't great at endearments. The love was there, but she didn't put it into speech. He thought that acting had cured her of showing love with words. Real love, not the stage variety.

'Dearest, this couldn't have anything to do with the Minden Street murders. They were too recent.'

Slowly Coffin said, 'I've always thought, I've known, there was another generation of death behind Minden Street.'

Stella, no cook – after all, you can't be a performer and a cook, and I am, she said to herself, a performer – had ordered in from their favoured restaurant a fine meal of roast duck, green peas and salad.

'Let's eat.'

They went through to the small dining room, whose window overlooked the theatre. Three theatres in fact, one of which was dark at present. The other two had big successes and royalty was coming to one for charity. Tickets were sold out.

This was an agreeable room, with white walls and golden

curtains. Stella studied herself in the large looking-glass on the wall opposite, where she could see that her latest extravagance, a silk trouser suit from a tailor who had worked at Prada, was probably a success. You had to be cautious, because you had to grow into clothes. The important thing, after a certain age, possibly any age, was to control waist and bottom. The bust didn't matter, because a good bra controlled it. Good meant expensive, she meditated. Her gaze flicked towards her husband, sitting there, face caught in a frown. Husbands had a risk factor too: waists were the trouble there. Fortunately, owing to the stresses of his life, Coffin lost weight rather than put it on, lucky thing.

There was a pucker on his mouth now.

'Wine all right?' she asked a little nervously. The wine was a claret; Coffin always said he was just a London copper who knew nothing about wine and had no palate, but he could be very testy if the wine did not come up to some invisible standard he had set for himself.

'Not bad at all.'

'I wondered about boiling it,' said Stella.

'Good idea,' said Coffin absently.

Stella started to laugh.

Coffin apologized. 'Sorry. The wine is splendid although perhaps better not boiled . . . I'm worried.'

'That much I had grasped.'

'I am sure I saw blood. Or a trace of it.' He got up.

'You're not going to look,' she protested.

He shook his head, taking out his mobile phone which he kept in his pocket; he liked to feel it was close. A neurosis? Probably. His responsibilities did weigh on him.

Stella shook her head. 'I never know if that thing is a good thing or a curse.' It sometimes seemed almost an extension of his body.

'You use yours often enough.' He was dialling a number. Stella watched him.

While he waited for the answer to his call, he studied her trouser suit. 'That's new, isn't it?'

Stella nodded. Well cut, expensive and made for her, that was the way to get good clothes, she thought. Anyway, after a certain age. She knew this splendid tailor for women (you had to have one who understood the female figure, or they got the legs and bottom wrong) and as a bonus there was a little shop nearby where you could buy a thick, rich, violet essence. Rose too, if you preferred rose, which she hardly ever did herself.

'I like it. If you'd told me before, I would have taken you out to show it off.' He put out his hand to her. There had been times in the not so distant past when their relationship had been troubled. Two hard-working, ambitious people, both pushing careers forward, sometimes left love aside.

There was a pause. 'The duck can wait. Won't spoil,' said Stella softly.

Then Phoebe's voice, deeper and huskier than usual, floated out of the telephone.

'Sir?' And into the silence, 'Sir? Phoebe Astley here. You called?'

Behind they could hear a female voice proclaiming it was a wrong number and not to answer.

'Is she still living with that girl who used to run a dress shop and then took a job in the theatre wardrobe?' Stella allowed herself this query, although she knew the answer was no.

'Oh, it's none of our business,' said Coffin irritably, in an aside.

'Can you hear a cat crying?' asked Stella.

'No,' said Coffin briefly. 'Phoebe? The Chief Commander here.'

As if I didn't know, thought Phoebe swiftly. And CC too, not just, 'Coffin here.' It's serious then. But it always was, one way and another, with him.

The voices in the background on both sides died away.

'I want you to get the forensics team down to the skulls under water. Also a photographer and SOCO.'

'But I thought,' began Phoebe . . . She could almost hear

18

Coffin saying, 'Don't think, just do as I say.' 'I thought the archaeologists wanted to be first,' she persevered.

'The forensics first, please, Phoebe. I think there may have been a crime.'

The conversation was over, as Phoebe recognized.

'No sex,' she said, turning towards her companion. 'No sex till morning.' And possibly not even then. 'Crime first.'

2

Thursday, on to Friday. Not Christmas yet,
maybe never.

Phoebe Astley said to the chief of forensics, Dr Hazzard, that yes, she often thought that the Chief Commander had precognition.

It was late evening, two days since she had passed on Coffin's request. She had done her bit, but she thought forensics had been slow.

'You took your time.'

'I had a lot on hand. If you remember there was a bad fire in a supermarket – several bodies could not be identified. All comes our way. Also, I had a moral obligation to let the archaeologist have a brief look to draw, map and photograph before anything was touched.'

But the forensics expert on what might now be called late-night duty, Dr George Hazzard, had delivered a tentative judgement. Dr Hazzard and Phoebe met professionally with some regularity. There had been a short but intense relationship between them when Phoebe first came to the Second City, the memory of which still hung over them like a cloud. A thundery one.

Almost put me off men for life, she thought. Almost. The question was still open, she was working on it. She did not count the Chief Commander as a man. He was *sui generis*, himself, unique. And just as well, possibly, as the possessor of precognitive powers.

21

Or the Chief Commander might just be a good guesser.

Without inspecting it closely, he had guessed that the 'different' skull was not as old as the others.

'Not by a long way,' said Dr Hazzard. 'I can't give a precise date. We'll need the pathologists and the medical chaps to help there.'

He was staring down at the skull, which had been carefully abstracted, under the watchful eye of one of the junior archaeologists, who took photographs and drew diagrams, leaving the other skulls in situ. The water was slowly draining away. And yes, Coffin had been right, there was a touch of blood on it, caught in a crack in the bone and therefore not washed away.

'Medical?' Phoebe was surprised. 'How new is it?'

Dr Hazzard smiled and shrugged. He liked to see his police colleagues taken aback.

Phoebe sought for words. 'Not contemporary?'

He shrugged again. 'It's an interesting question. Age and provenance. Where did it come from, and how? I like that sort of a problem.'

'It's not a game.'

'Who said it was?'

'You know what I mean: if the skull is beyond a certain age, then there's no case to worry CID.' She looked hopefully, then speculatively, at Hazzard who appeared to be thinking. Provoking bugger, she thought.

After a quiet second, taking a deep breath, he said: 'I think CID might have a case.'

'What was the age of the owner of this skull? It is a baby's skull, I suppose.'

'Oh yes, I think so. But we will have to get the medical pathologist in on this to help us date and age the skull.'

'So how long has it been in the water?'

'Possibly not so very long. I am still guessing a bit.'

'Yes, I can see that.' And enjoying it. 'I suppose I shouldn't call the skull "it". A person once. A baby person. Maybe not so long ago either.'

She looked at Hazzard, a nice man at heart, even if the heart had to be excavated. 'Couldn't you make a guess?'

'I could guess . . . don't hold me to it.'

'Out with it. Let me have it.'

'The skull might be recent,' Hazzard said carefully. 'Contemporary, possibly. Tests will show.'

'How contemporary?'

Hazzard was silent.

'Where did the hair and flesh go? The child had hair and flesh.'

Hazzard remained silent. Then he said hesitantly, 'It could have been . . . treated.'

We'll have to talk about this, thought Phoebe. Meanwhile, a cold shiver ran through her.

'So what was the age of this dead child?' She was determined to get more of an answer than she had done so far.

Hazzard put his head on one side. 'Not my sphere. You'll have to ask a paediatrician or some such.'

He kept saying that; she was getting tetchy.

'Guess.'

'Very young,' he allowed. 'Weeks only.'

'Infanticide then.' Phoebe said heavily.

'We don't know that. The child may have died naturally. Even been born dead.'

'So the child was as young as that?'

'Just could be. You'll have to get an expert in that field to be sure. Which I am not.'

'Took a long time to shell that out of you,' said Phoebe. 'Put it in writing, will you?' she added vindictively. She knew he hated writing reports. Well, who didn't, but it was part of the job. She took a certain pleasure in handing this one out. 'I will let the Chief Commander know. It won't be a surprise to him, he must have suspected it.'

'Clever fellow.'

He is that, thought Phoebe. 'I don't know what sort of enquiry will be started.' Coffin wouldn't leave it there.

Whose baby's head was it? Why was it there in the pit

with the Neanderthal babies? And what had been done to the skull?

He would ask all those questions and want answers.

Likewise, where was the body?

She was so deep in these thoughts as she walked Dr Hazzard to his car that she failed to notice his troubled, thoughtful face.

He had noticed something about the infant head.

Next day, in his own office, with the rain beating on the windows, Coffin received the news in silence.

Phoebe had come to see him herself, making a late-afternoon appointment and keeping scrupulously to the minute.

'Hazzard thinks the head may have been boiled.' She saw his look of comprehension. 'Or stewed, to get rid of the flesh and the hair and create a skull. There is a little hair left.'

'Oh God.'

There was something pathetic and terrible enough about infanticide without this extra horror.

He had had plenty to think about as he had studied the papers in the files on his desk, took the various telephone calls that constantly interrupted his reading, and looked at his e-mail. Letters too, all opened with a noted observation on them for his secretary. Not all opened. Still there, one last letter, which he did not want to open at this time full of murderous thoughts.

The Minden Street murders, Jack Jackson and the missing Mrs Lumsden. If she was missing. Pray God, she might yet come back. Phoebe Astley was in charge of the Minden Street murders, and Sergeant Drury was attending to Arthur Lumsden and his missing wife. Why not let them get on with it?

He was alone all day in his office in the big dusty building in the Second City. In the outer offices, of which there were two, were his secretaries – he had two of them, as well as his personal assistant, Paul Masters. There was a constant staff turnover. The days of devoted assistants who stayed for ever were gone; ambition brought people to work with him (he was the source of power, wasn't he?) and then dragged them on and up. He was never sure what this building had been before the Second City and his Force were created. Sometimes he had thought it must have been a school, one of the solid, typecast Victorian erections in which the poorer classes were imprisoned to be educated: babies on the ground floor, then mixed-sex older children, then senior girls on the top. Senior boys, being dangerous, were weeded out at this stage and sent off to a separate building.

In addition there was the blunt-faced, architect-designed new building where most of the staff worked. He preferred the old part, liking the sense of history, even the dust of ages that came with it. Whatever history it was.

Or was he imagining all this? Possibly the building had been the head offices of some shipping company from the days when the docks were full of ocean-going steamers.

He had once asked Sir Harold Bottome, the Chief Administrator of the Second City, a kind of perpetual Lord Mayor, a gentle but much harried man. Sir Harold had looked vague. 'Don't know, my dear chap, the present of this bloody Second City is as much as I can keep up with, but I will send you some of the history books with pictures.' He had done so and Stella had read them and said there was nothing about Coffin's HQ being a school and she guessed it had always been a police building. If not a prison.

Of course, now he knew that a group of Neanderthals had lived and died here, it helped him have a feeling for the place.

'Is Hazzard sure of this?'

'No, not sure, he wants to take advice.'

Coffin nodded. 'Give me news, when you get it.' What a world. 'Makes you feel sick, doesn't it?'

Then he thanked Phoebe. Clearly, she expected something.

'We can't leave it there,' she said.

'No, indeed.' He was going to put the job on her shoulders but he was thinking of a way to tell her. Issuing orders to Phoebe, which as her chief he was certainly able to do, could make her very awkward indeed.

'I haven't said anything, but somehow the local paper has got hold of it.'

'It's a good story, you can't blame them . . . Makes the flesh creep a bit. Or is your flesh too strong?'

Phoebe laughed. 'No, creeps with the best.'

'Phoebe, you are the only person I can think of at the moment who can handle this.'

Phoebe knew blandishment when she heard it. 'I've got a lot on, you know. It's not just the Minden Street killings.'

'Who knows that better than I do? But it's the job, Phoebe. Crimes don't come just when it suits us and we are free to handle them. You know what Bernard Shaw said about *Romeo and Juliet*? He said it was "all butchers and bones". Crime is like that, hard but true. You know it as well as I do. All working policemen know it.'

The Force in the Second City had grown since Coffin had taken over, but it was now under financial pressure. It had expanded, but must now contract, and do all the same work, if not more.

Blood and bones, thought Phoebe; the Minden Street murders were like that. She had gone to inspect the dead with the SOCO before they were moved. She closed her eyes for a second, shutting out Coffin's worried face (he was wearing spectacles for the first time, she noted, and distantly she thought she could hear him explaining how pressed they were), and seeing the dead sisters, Amy and Alice, on the floor of the hall, blood everywhere, and the bones . . . For a moment she could hardly bear to recall it . . . the bones of arms and legs showing white where a bullet had torn through the flesh. The mother had had her throat penetrated by a bullet so that her backbone showed. Who had hated them so much?

'You all right, Phoebe?' Coffin's voice cut into her.

'Yes, sure,' Phoebe answered quickly. 'It was just the thing about bones.'

There was a moment of silence.

'Yes, I'll do it. Or do what I can. The rape business is almost tidied up. I think the girl was lying, and it was sex by consent, and she is on the point of admitting it. But I will need some more hands with the the Minden Street case.' Grab what you can, when you can, a hard little voice inside her said.

'I'll see what we can do,' said Coffin, almost humbly for him.

'You do realize we may never learn about the baby? In fact, most likely not.' She decided to get on to Dr Murray to see what help she could give.

He nodded. 'Let's do what we can for the poor little soul . . . the Neanderthal babies . . . well, that's too far away and long ago.'

Phoebe looked down at her shoes, noticing that she had put on odd black and brown ones. It showed her state of mind: busy and overworked, and more than lightly involved with a new love.

'I'll be off.'

Coffin nodded and saw her to the door, still talking. 'You know, all these cases touch me in my own person: the baby, the Minden Street murders . . . that's because of Stella, and Arthur Lumsden, because I've been a copper and plodded the street and had trouble with a wife.'

Had he said all that aloud to Phoebe? He hoped he hadn't.

On his desk there was the one last letter that he had not yet opened. The envelope, crisp and white, was handwritten.

He now opened and read it. Then he made a telephone call.

'Archie? Glad to get you. The letter you told me about has arrived. And the answer is yes.'

He bought some flowers for Stella from Mimsie Marker on the way home.

Mimsie's stall outside Spinnergate tube station had expanded over the last year.

'You could live off all this, Mimsie,' he said looking around at hot coffee, cold drinks from a mini-fridge, hot dogs, sandwiches, croissants and delicious-looking cakes. 'The newspapers are getting squeezed out.'

'People don't read like they used to,' said Mimsie sadly. Then she smiled radiantly. 'But they eat, so I diversified.'

Coffin chose roses and irises and big narcissi; he had no idea where Mimsie got her flowers – possibly she went to the New Covent Garden Market herself – but her flowers were always fresh and lovely.

He hesitated, wondering whether to talk to her about the Minden Street killings. She'd have an opinion, because she always did.

But she got there first. 'Miss Pinero'll miss the Jackson twins.' She didn't wait for him to answer. 'Mind you, I can't believe the brother did it. I didn't like the man, who could, although most of the things he claimed to fancy doing, I never believed in. One of those fellers who likes to be thought wicked. Not the only one I've known. A bit of an actor.'

'He had a key,' said Coffin. 'Looks as though whoever killed them had a key.'

Mimsie nodded and pursed her lips, but all she said was, 'See the flowers have a good drink.'

Stella was already at home when he got back. In the beginning of his life in the Second City he had just had one flat, but as money got easier and Stella became his wife, the whole tower became their home. Stella had made it beautiful, elegant, liveable, with a slight yet attractive touch of theatricality. She came up to him and kissed him on the cheek.

'You're actually home when you said you would be. And with flowers. Beautiful ones.' She carried the bunch through to the kitchen, where she began to arrange them in a crystal vase.

Coffin followed her in. 'Mimsie says the flowers need a good drink.'

'She always says that. And I always take it she means water, not black coffee followed by a strong brandy.'

For once, Coffin did not laugh at her little joke. 'Have you got dinner arranged?'

Stella opened her mouth to explain, no, not really, not yet, but . . .

Before she could speak, Coffin said, 'Let's go to eat at that place in Greenwich that we both like . . . I can ring up and book a table. And then we can go for a drive.'

Stella opened her mouth, but once again Coffin got in first, 'It's stopped raining, and there's a moon.'

She could see in his face that he wanted to go. 'Greenwich it is then.' She was not always a sympathetic wife but she was one who could read his face. 'Farmers?'

'Yes, I feel like a nice straightforward English meal.'

Farmers was a small restaurant not far from Greenwich Park that they had discovered together. It had a faithful and discriminatory clientele.

'We haven't been for a bit. We used to take Gus there.'

'When he was up to it.'

'Oh, he will be again.' Gus was the dear old dog who had just undergone a triple bypass in the local pet clinic, his heart attack brought on, so they thought, from shock at finding the body of their cat, who died peacefully and quietly in Gus's bed. Coffin's bed too, as it happened.

'They liked him and brought him his special meal on a special dish. And he could eat under the table if he was quiet. They'll remember us.'

They'll remember you all right, thought Stella. The last time you were in there you went away to a quiet corner and on your mobile phone arranged the arrest of one of our fellow diners. He went quietly too, no trouble to anyone.

'If I see you pick up your mobile, I shall scream. Loudly.'

Coffin smiled at her. He knew Stella had a good, strong, theatrical scream. Learnt, so she said, from Edith Evans.

'I'd forgotten that episode.'

'No, you haven't. You never forget anything.' Except anniversaries and my first nights. 'But it's why we haven't been there for some time.' But he grinned; they knew each other well enough and had loved each other long enough to know when to laugh. It was one of the reasons their union had survived.

'I will now admit that I hoped that man, Jordan, would be there when I suggested we eat there.'

Stella absorbed this, but said nothing until they were on the way there, driving through the tunnel. 'So, what's planned for this evening? Don't tell me it's just the pleasure of my company?'

'Trust me.'

'Did you book a table?'

'No. They'll squeeze us in, I'm sure. Let's go for a drive first.'

This was the second occasion he had mentioned going for a drive through South London, but Stella did not say so.

The streets were not crowded with traffic, but there were delivery lorries, the odd bus, private cars, none very new or smart, all edging forward.

Through Greenwich and into Deptford, down Evelyn Street and towards Rotherhithe.

'I miss the docks,' said Coffin. 'And the sound of the ships on the river.' He was driving slowly. 'Of course, it's not a working river any more, not upriver anyway.'

Stella kept silent.

'It was all flooded down here once . . . Every twenty-five years they fear a flood.'

'Should be due one soon,' said Stella. 'Who was it said that this part of England sinks a centimetre every year?' She sounded comfortably unbelieving.

'There's the Thames barrier now. With that in place, statistically it should be one thousand, five hundred years before a huge tide comes over the top.'

'You can't believe in figures,' said a sceptical Stella. '*Après moi le déluge* . . . Who said that? Some king, wasn't it?'

'He must have been a French king,' Coffin answered absently. He had turned the car before it got into Bermondsey and was driving back. 'I used to live down here once . . . Just wanted to look around. All changed. Great big housing blocks instead of little streets.'

'What is all this about, love?'

'I had a feeling I wanted to see all these streets again. Nostalgia, I suppose.'

And something else, she thought. You are sad about something. Those infants' skulls?

Across the river, in the streets that they had left behind them, the University of the Second City had all its lights on because a number of its students worked all day and studied at night. The Second City now had three universities, but the USC (which was how students and staff spoke of it) was the most crowded. As with the police Headquarters, it was made up of older buildings and very new ones. Cleaning was done on a shoestring because money for books was accepted as more important, which meant that some of the older buildings, if they had a voice, would have cried out: Remember me, here I am, give me a dust.

Also attached was the Second City University Hospital, which had an important role since it was an old establishment with a long history of teaching and training doctors and nurses. It was very academic.

Joseph Bottom, deputy head cleaner, did a lot of extra work, some in the hospital, some in the university proper, without worrying about it. He was proud of working in the University Hospital, so close to the university itself, where his elder daughter was now an assistant professor. Joe was a tall, thick-set man in whom so many nationalities had come together over the generations, London near the docks and the ships in the old days being that sort of city; he used to call himself a walking advertisement for the United Nations. His daughter Flora had creamy dark skin, red hair and bright blue eyes, and was one of the beauties of the university, much loved by her students. She liked work, as did Joe, and both of them worked as many hours as they chose to get the job done. They were death to union rules.

Joe, a great colonizer, had turned a cupboard-like room into the rest room for him and his assistants. He had painted it white but his helpers had covered the walls with graffiti and advertisements that took their eye. Some advertisements tactfully or blatantly (depending on the publication) offered high wages for anything up to and including what sounded like gun-running or the odd quiet murder.

It was, of course, recognized that professors and doctors worked all hours and no one questioned it, but when Joe took his cleaning equipment into what he called the 'museum of bones' it was a bit on the late side. On a less busy day he might have been having a drink in his local or cooking his wife a supper. She was a nurse who worked even harder than he did and for less pay.

All the same, he would have been glad to have had the help of his assistant Sam, who hadn't shown his face.

'Not here, as usual . . . bloody loafer.' When Joe had said he could have this job, Sam had replied that there was always work for a man, which Joe knew to be only half a truth.

Sam was efficient when he turned up, but he claimed bad health. Big, dark-skinned and burly, and not much of a talker. Not Joe's favourite chap, but he felt he must look after him, goodness knows why, it was just the effect Sam had on some people. 'Ask him to supper and get the wife to cook one of her meat pies. Don't think Sam feeds himself.' Sam Brother lived in a small flat, built by the local council, in almost sensuous disarray. Joe would swear the cooker was never used. He drove himself around on an ancient motorbike that he kept in good repair; he was said to love it more than any woman. Not that Joe had ever seen him with a woman. Only dogs and the odd cat. He had a way with animals.

He threw open the door of the museum of bones, which was, in fact, a smallish room lined with cabinets that exhibited human bones illustrating medical conditions.

It was not much frequented, since medics don't do things that way any longer; they have scans, and X-rays and hardly need to look at the human frame any more. But he supposed the odd medical man came in sometimes. He had a key himself, of course.

As he advanced into the room, he gave a shout and seized his broom, his only weapon of defence since a vacuum cleaner is no help at all. Someone had broken open the cabinets, shattering the glass doors and throwing bones and skulls all around. There was glass on the ground and a body at his feet. A circle of small skulls had been arranged around the head.

'They didn't get there by accident,' decided Joe.

Joe was a great reader of detective novels and he knew he wanted the police. More, he wanted John Coffin, whom he had heard give a lecture on Crime and the Second City. A policeman who had a wife like Stella Pinero was the one for him.

'Get John Coffin,' he said aloud, looking down at the victim.

There wasn't a female version of victim, like 'victime' or 'victima', but this one was definitely a woman.

He saw her lips move. 'Coffin,' she seemed to say. 'Yes, yes.' An echo of his words, or her last wish?

Then she stopped. Death had silenced her.

Mr Jones of Farmers Restaurant received them with a smile and showed them at once to a table in a corner. In spite of what he had said Coffin must have rung up and booked a table.

Stella shook her head at her husband. Mr Jones saw it and looked anxious.

'You prefer somewhere else?'

'No, this is just right,' said Stella.

'I thought it was what Mr Coffin wanted.'

'It is,' said Coffin speedily. 'Just what I wanted. Have you got a bottle of that good Sancerre?' Then he responded to

Stella's raised eyebrows. 'When you were putting on fresh lipstick and some more scent.'

'I didn't think you noticed.'

'I always notice.'

'So?'

'I know that the death of the Jackson twins has distressed you.'

Stella looked down at her hands. One way or another her life with Coffin had brought her close to death, sometimes too close.

'They were only kids.' Sometimes she felt that being married to a man like Coffin brought death into the family. 'Don't let's talk about it now. Later.' The best solution was to think of herself as a character in a play, a bit of fiction, and the deaths the same, nothing real.

He took a drink. 'I had a letter today. It came this morning, but I opened it just before I came out.'

Stella looked at him.

'It was from Sally Young. About their baby.'

Stella nodded.

'She enclosed a letter from Charlie. He wrote it just before he was killed. Didn't have a chance to post it. He wrote it just after he'd seen the scan on the child. He already knew he had a son. He rang up his father and asked if it would be all right to ask me to act as godfather.' He took a swig of wine. 'Archie said yes, of course. Hence the letter. Sally held on to it for a while, and now she has posted it. The christening is next week.'

'You'll be godfather, of course.'

'You'll help me, Stella, won't you? I can't do it without your help.' He held out the letter. 'Read it.'

Stella read it slowly, then she looked up at her husband. 'He admired you – you were a good copper. Straight. He doesn't use the word integrity, but he means it. He wants the boy to have that. He says he knows you can't really teach it, but you can show it.' She put the letter carefully in his hand. 'It's a great compliment he paid you.'

'A painful one.'

Stella considered it. 'I think the best ones often are, because they have a truth tucked away inside that can hurt. It's the other side of a compliment.'

'That's a bit too profound for me,' said Coffin, who suspected she had made it up that moment to cheer him up.

'I read it somewhere, I think,' said Stella, confirming his suspicion.

They were halfway through their meal, after the clear soup and enjoying the roast beef, when Coffin heard his mobile trilling away in his pocket.

Phoebe's voice always rang out loud and clear so that Stella could hear every word she said. As, probably, could the couple at the next table.

'Sir,' said Phoebe. 'It's about the head . . . the head that was different.'

The couple heard that all right, but pretended not to.

'The infant's skull. We now know where it came from. Sex isn't clear yet. Nor cause of death.'

That took the couple's mind off their smoked salmon. Coffin also had noticed the attention the next table was giving his conversation. 'Go on.'

Something in his tone must have told Phoebe she was shouting, because her voice dropped so that even Stella could only catch odd words.

'University . . . museum . . . specimen not noticed.'

Then Phoebe's voice became audible again. 'Yes, sir. I have Inspector Dover with me, this being his patch . . . There's no need for you to come, but I thought you would want to know.'

Coffin put his mobile on the table, then looked at his wife.

'Eat up, Stella,' he said.

3

Friday evening.

Joe stood waiting quietly for the arrival of the Chief Commander. Phoebe Astley, whom he knew – they bought their meat and sausages from the same butcher, of whom there were not many left around, even in the Second City – had told him to wait. He stood looking out of the window on to the street lights below. It was raining, but it had its own romance.

'I love London,' he said to himself. 'I am a Londoner. Perhaps I'm not an Englishman.' Too much mixed blood. 'But I am a Londoner.'

This part of London too, the Second City – not Knightsbridge nor Piccadilly, you could have that bit – this was his London.

He was not ambitious, although his daughter was, which he thought was as it should be. It was all right for men like him to slop around in old clothes and take undemanding jobs – you didn't need a degree in engineering to dust a floor. He was a man, anyway, and that had to count for something. Women had to try harder.

'Mustn't get too sentimental, Joseph,' he told himself. 'There's a dead woman in this room and she didn't put herself there.' He had never been so close to a dead person before, not one untouched by medical hands and neatly trussed up so that they became someone you had never known.

He had known the dead woman too, and had even heard her dying words.

*   *   *

Phoebe Astley came back into the room, bringing the Chief Commander with her. Inspector Dover followed behind. His usual spot. She nodded at Joe.

'I know who you are, sir,' said Joe quickly, before Chief Inspector Astley – hard to think of her as that and not as rump steak, ostrich liver if you have any, and some pork sausages – could give him another of those quick nods and get rid of him. Although he was not an ambitious man, he had a link-up with the local newspaper who printed any little items of news and gossip he sent to them. Working where and how he did, he picked up quite a lot. Behind a Hoover, you were not there.

Coffin was not listening.

Joe took a step back. He didn't even need a Hoover to be invisible, he told himself.

Coffin studied the woman. This terrible task didn't take more than a minute. 'It's Dr Murray.'

Phoebe nodded. 'It is.'

'Anyone had a look at her?'

Dover answered. 'The police surgeon who certified her death.' He nodded towards Joe. 'And Joe here found her. He called the university security office, who called the police. Sergeant Fermer came, and I followed.'

Coffin looked at Phoebe with a question.

'I came into it because I had been interested in the Neanderthal skulls. She was interested in the skulls . . .'

He nodded. 'Yes, I know.'

'Anyway, she had my name and rank on a bit of paper in her handbag.'

Coffin went to stare again at the body. He knelt down, but did not touch her. A band of blood, like a red ribbon, ran down the face, spreading out to cover the nose and then the chin. The hair was clotted with blood. Her grey tweed skirt and matching jacket were stained too. Blood had even spattered her shoes.

'She could have been hit on the head.' He got up. 'First, before the rest, but I don't think so. The medics will tell us.

It looks as if someone took her by surprise.'

'No weapon found,' said Phoebe tersely. 'Just in case you wondered.'

'She never came in here. No one did,' said Joe, not loudly but suddenly, as if he had just thought of it. 'In all the years I've cleaned this place, I've never seen anyone. It's kind of forgotten, this place.' He turned his short-sighted blue eyes on the Chief Commander and CI Astley. 'She asked for you, sir. With her dying breath, she asked for you.'

Coffin took it in but did not know whether to believe it: people caught up in violent death had such fantasies.

Probably the worst fantasy of all was that he would be of any use.

He looked around at the floor, at all the skeletal remains that lay about which the killer had abstracted from the cabinets and then thrown all over the floor, except for the skulls, where a pattern had been made.

Or had the dead woman herself taken them out?

No, the little skulls, babies' skulls, were arranged round her own head. Certainly she had not done that herself.

'What the hell do the bones and skulls mean?'

Phoebe didn't answer.

'No, you don't know it any more than I do. But whoever did this was angry.'

The SOCO team arrived.

'You took your time,' Coffin said crisply.

'Traffic, sir, sorry,' said the team leader, far from pleased to see the Chief Commander there. Traffic as an excuse was the first thing he could think of. Not strictly true; a bit of an argument between two of the team had slowed them down. He could see by the look in the Chief Commander's eyes that he was not believed. If I'd known it was you here waiting for us, I'd have been quicker. But the top brass never knew how those down below felt. There had been a lot of irritation lately, partly because of the new building works, which had meant shuffling people around. The skulls were objects of interest, and yet of disquiet too. The water had drained away so that the archaeologists had been at work, measuring and photographing. Then some other police teams had arrived. Men from the scientific side.

Coffin said, 'It's now early evening. I want to know when she was killed. Also, how anyone could get in here. Was it usually kept locked or not? And anything that forensics can turn up.'

'Are you taking over, sir?' Phoebe kept her voice polite, although she was irritated by him.

'No. You are. But I will be behind you.'

Behind and in front and in the air above, thought Phoebe. No one who has worked with him has ever exactly been left alone. And yet we all like the bugger. Did I really call him that in my mind? I shouldn't have done, because he is always polite, sometimes gentle, even at his most ruthless.

'Check these skulls . . . what is known about them, who uses them and for what purpose.'

'A medical purpose, I judge,' said Phoebe.

'Dr Murray was not a doctor but an archaeologist.' But he had answered his own question. Archaeologists dealt in bones too.

He remembered her face as she had looked at that odd little skull with the water washing over it. She had been troubled. No, not exactly troubled: thoughtful, knowing. She had known something about that infant skull.

Coffin knew nothing about infant craniums, and some of those encircling Margaret Murray's head looked very, very small, and others looked odd.

He knew nothing, but there were those that did.

'Get a doctor, preferably a paediatrician, to look at these heads and tell me what he says.'

Joe said, 'You don't need a doctor.' But once again he was invisible.

Stella had been left sitting in the car. For a while she was patient, but this patience did not last. She took a deep breath, got out of the car, remembered to lock it, and marched into the hospital building.

She didn't know where her husband was, nor did she know her way around. One hospital may be much like another one, but you still have to know the signs: no, not the signs that tell you this way to Ear, Nose and Throat Department, or Pharmacy This Way, or Operating Theatre X, Third Floor, but the flow of people, the sense of urgency. A hospital was in a way like a theatre, she thought: the cutting edge, those in charge, otherwise the surgeons and nurses, and the audience, otherwise the suffering, the patients.

I must have drunk more than I realized, she thought. Surely not, I drank very little, and anyway on occasion I have a stronger head than my husband. Depends on emotion. If you are really down, you drink the bottles empty but never get high, but if you are happy half a glass can do it.

So she must have been happy; it was one way of telling.

A hand touched her shoulder. She swung round. A large young woman, fat really, but pretty, carrying a folder of documents or they might have been photographs; you were always getting photographed or X-rayed in hospitals. Or so it seemed in the sort of films and TV soaps that Stella watched, when she watched. Or acted in.

'Oh, Joanna.'

'Yes, Joanna. You were looking down at your shoes so hard that you didn't notice an old friend.'

'I was trying to make up my mind about them. Someone said they were kinky.'

'Kinky?'

Joanna studied what Stella was wearing: the shoes were black patent, shiny, high-heeled, with just a hint of something in the white line that ran round the toe.

'That person was not a friend,' said Joanna severely. 'Stella, you could never be called kinky, nor anything you wear. Even by putting them on, those shoes ceased to be kinky.'

Stella looked at Joanna with caution. She was never sure when Joanna was laughing at her. She probably was doing so now, but never mind, she was glad to see her. If surprised.

'You work here now?'

'In accounts.'

'Oh yes, you always were into figures.'

They looked at each other and laughed. The two had met in the early days when Stella was working in Greenwich and Joanna Kinnear was taking her final exams in accountancy, and they met again when she had discovered that Joanna was doing the accounts for the private hospital that had attended to Stella's facial requirements (mention not the words 'uplift' and 'beauty surgery'). And now here she was in a big hospital, wearing a white coat and looking important. She probably was.

Joanna saw her look. 'Even hospitals have bills and accounts to keep,' she said with amusement. 'In fact, they are big spenders.'

'Why are you wearing a white coat, though?'

'Oh, I just like to look a big shot.'

Stella accepted the explanation while not believing it. She knew enough about modern hospitals to know that white coats were out of fashion, laundry costs presumably. No, there was more behind it than Joanna was saying, but not for Stella to enquire.

'I've lost my husband.'

'Medically, or emotionally?'

'Practically. He came in to see a skull . . . a baby's skull.'

'Oh, the dead babies' room.' A nerve twitched in her cheek, as if it wanted to be scratched. Stella felt she wanted to scratch it for her, but you don't scratch anyone's face for them.

'What?'

'That's what we call it.' She put out her hand. For a moment, Stella thought she was going to scratch that itch, which was still twitching away, but no, the hand was being offered to her.

'Come, I'll take you there.'

Down a long corridor, and then a right turn, and across a courtyard.

Of course, museums are always in bloody awkward places, thought Stella, picking her way across the uneven paving stones. If she broke an ankle, as seemed likely, at least she was in the right place to get it fixed.

A uniformed constable stood outside double glass doors, surveying them blankly. He was a new recruit, fresh in the Second City; he thought he might know Stella's face, which reminded him of a television drama he had watched, as indeed it might, since Stella had performed in it. The other woman he definitely did not know, but in his opinion she was too tall to be a woman, although well built.

'Oh, dear,' said Joanna. 'Trouble. Might have guessed it, since your husband is here.'

'Thank you,' said Stella.

She addressed herself to the constable. 'I am Mrs Coffin. I want to speak to my husband.'

The constable's blank expression did not change. Intensified rather.

'She is,' said Joanna. 'I can swear to it.'

Now there was doubt in his face.

'I'll be off,' said Joanna. 'Give me a ring.' Over her shoulder, she called. 'Take my advice: break in.'

The alarmed young officer advanced towards Stella. She was saved by the door swinging open to let Sergeant Dawlish pass through.

'Hello, Mrs Coffin. Can I help you?'

'Can I see my husband?'

'He's a bit tied up at the moment.'

A comment that Stella rightly interpreted as meaning her husband did not want to see anyone, not on the job. Not even her.

Coffin called, 'Is that Dr Merchant?'

When he saw Stella, his face changed.

'You forgot me.'

'No.' He took a step forward. 'Don't come in, love.'

But she was already level with him at the great swing doors and could see beyond. Her view of the body was blocked by the police photographer busily taking pictures of the dead woman and the place of her death. Although she could not see the face, she could see the shoes and knew it was a woman lying there.

'Who is she?'

Coffin did not answer.

'That means it's someone I know.'

Coffin gave a little shake of his head.

'That didn't say yes and didn't say no,' complained Stella sharply, but inside herself she was saying, By God, yes it did. I know this dead person, dead woman, I know it's a woman . . . But who is it?

Ignoring her husband, she pushed past him into the room. 'Who is this doctor you thought I was?'

Coffin muttered something about skulls, a paediatrician.

Stella had taken a pace within the room. She could see the half a dozen or so skulls that had been made into a macabre ring round the dead woman's head.

'Doctor . . .' she said scornfully. 'You don't need a doctor. I don't know what this doctor will tell you, but I would have thought you could have seen for yourself.'

'Each of these little creatures was malformed . . . no normal baby has a skull like that.'

Dr Merchant came strolling up with the ease of one who knows that there is no hurry. All his specimens were dead.

'Mr Coffin, I am sorry if I kept you waiting . . . I had to come across from the university, a committee meeting.' He looked around him. 'I am the curator of this little museum, one of my subsidiary jobs. The Jordan Jones Museum, a Victorian doctor and donor. Not much used now, ways have changed, but he left a bit of cash too.' He gave a half-smile, 'But I see you managed all right without me.'

Coffin said tersely, possibly with a touch of grimness, 'We managed.'

44

Merchant advanced to look. 'Poor soul, poor soul. How was she discovered?'

Joe had found her in fact and called security, but Phoebe preferred to put it her way. 'We had arranged to meet here.' Phoebe Astley was short.

Merchant looked his question.

'She was helping me with my enquiries.'

'Poor woman, poor woman. And yet, you know, you could almost have predicted a violent death for her. There are some people like that. And if they miss it one way, then they get it another.'

'You know who she is?'

Dr Merchant almost gave a friendly smile. 'Of course. There is no more efficient gossip mill than a hospital.' He added, half thoughtfully, 'Her husband cuts my hair.' He ran his hand over his designer trim, layered and shaped. Everyone has his own vanity.

'You know him?' asked Phoebe Astley.

'He does some private work, out of the Mayfair salon. Just the cut and the styling. Calls himself a man with a knife and a pair of scissors.' Then he realized what he had said, and added hastily, 'I'm sure it was a very happy marriage and he will be devastated. Does he know yet?'

Phoebe did not answer. She had no idea. Somewhere in Spinnergate, no doubt the uniformed men would be dealing with that part, might already have done so.

'He might not be there, of course,' went on Ken Merchant. 'He's away a lot. Demonstrations and photographic sessions.'

You seem to know a lot about him, thought Coffin, who had been silently observing the scene and realizing that Phoebe not only knew Dr Merchant, or of him (he'd have to think that one over), but also didn't like him. Might be worth finding out.

This view was confirmed when, moving forward to thank Dr Merchant for coming, he gave him the polite dismissal and said that Chief Inspector Astley would be taking his statement. He saw the look of satisfaction flit across Phoebe's face. What had he done to her?

'Statement?' No pleasure there, instead surprise and hurt dignity.

'Just routine,' Phoebe assured him. 'Anyone who has access to the museum.' She murmured something about fingerprints with some satisfaction.

He must have either spurned her or raped her, thought Coffin. He did not usually form such wicked witticisms about a colleague and friend, but even he sometimes had a thought better not expressed that he pressed firmly down, and this one had escaped.

He realized he was in shock.

Stella meanwhile had performed the well-known theatrical trick of disappearing while still being there. (She could do the opposite too: not being there but seeming to be present, while really being at the hairdresser's having a tint.)

'I'll clear off,' said Dr Merchant. 'Leave you to it. I'll be in my room working, if you want me. I am preparing a lecture for tomorrow. Room 3A in the Bedford teaching block.'

'Thank you,' said Coffin, his eyes on the group round the body. However often you saw it and however tough you were, there was something final about the journey to the pathologist's table.

'Ready to move her now,' said Phoebe Astley.

Something rolled from the body, out of a pocket in her jacket.

Golden, round and shining. It was a wedding ring.

'Were the clothes searched?' Coffin found himself unable to say 'her' clothes . . . too personal, better keep it neutral.

'Not really, sir,' said Dover. 'A quick search to establish identity . . . The rest will be done by forensics when the clothes come off.' Subdued hint of reproof here: You know the ropes, sir.

Coffin knew them. To Phoebe Astley, he said, 'Keep me up to date.'

'I will, of course.'

Underneath, they were conducting a different dialogue. Coffin was saying that this was a particularly bloody murder in which he had been named and called in, and he wanted to know why.

From Phoebe, proving that great minds do not necessarily think alike, came the thought that she was irritated by this and wished he would keep out. She would call him when it was necessary.

Coffin picked up the irritation as he watched the body removed.

'What about the MO?' he asked Phoebe. 'Does it remind you of the Minden Street murders?'

Phoebe shrugged. 'We don't know if she even knew where Minden Street was.'

'Minden Street may have known where she was.' He was pacing the area where the body had rested.

Plenty of blood. Too much. Amazing the way the heart keeps pumping it out when it would be better to stop. Even if help had got there earlier, she would probably still have died.

And she had asked for him, allegedly. By name.

Coffin. Get Coffin. Sounded like a Hitchcock film.

To Phoebe he said, 'Get the blood tested.'

Surprised, Phoebe nodded. 'We always do, sir.'

Coffin walked round the room. The police technicians, still at work, moved aside as he came past.

It was a small museum, showing not only heads. Whole skeletons, exposed in the old-fashioned cabinets, had not been disturbed.

'It's the heads that are important,' he said, coming back to Phoebe.

Looking at the ring of tiny skulls, Phoebe thought she had worked that out for herself.

'Question the man Joe thoroughly. I get the feeling he may know something.'

'That will be done, sir.'

'I'll go to the post-mortem with you,' said Coffin. He felt

he should; the dead woman had asked for him as she died. It was the least he could do for her.

'Thanks. I hate that place.'

'So do I.' Who didn't? As a young policeman he had attended post-mortems as duty demanded. He hated the ice cabinets, with their freight of bodies, the trays on which they emerged to lie on metal tables with drip trays underneath.

Coffin looked round for Stella, only to find that she had done a disappearing act, and not a theatrical one; she was nowhere to be seen.

She was outside in the car, reading.

'I shall always bring a book with me when you take me out to dinner, then I can read it when you go off.'

'You seem to have got one.'

'I found it in the car.' She held it up: *David Copperfield*. 'I never had you down as a Dickens reader.'

'Oh, every one is at some point . . .' He could see this needed amplification. 'I thought Dickens' London might help me with the Second City.'

'And has it?'

'Not really. Some of the characters fit in. Mimsie Marker, for instance. She'd be the rich eccentric who rescues the lost child.'

'And you would be the poor little lost boy, I suppose?'

Coffin was quiet. Maybe yes, maybe no.

As he started the car, Phoebe went past, gave them a wave. No smile.

'What's up with her?'

'Oh, she's having an identity crisis. She has them at times.'

'Sex?'

'That too, I expect.'

As he spoke, Phoebe came back. 'I'll see the blood is tested.' Then she said, 'I'll go and see the cousin, Natasha Broad. Do you want to come, sir?'

'As Dr Murray asked for me by name, I think I had better.'

'I'll set it up and call for you, sir.'

'Right.'

'Better be soon, I think, don't you?'

'Have to be. If not soon, then not at all. She has someone with her?'

'There's a husband.'

As they drove away, Stella said, 'Did you go and call on the Jacksons?'

'No. There was no one left to call on.'

All dead.

Bar one. Jack. But that would be attended to. 'Funny you should ask. I had been thinking about them, and I believe Phoebe was too.'

'You think the same person killed Dr Murray?'

'Could be. It's not impossible. That's why I want forensics to get a move on.'

'You mean the way she was killed? The gunshot?'

'Yes.' He had meant that, but in addition it came to him that there had been a smell. A sour, body smell, as if the killer had run a long way to the kill and hung about afterwards so that he had left his ghost behind.

Without meaning to, Coffin put his foot down.

'You're driving much too fast,' reproved Stella.

It was true he had visited the house in Minden Street and seen the bodies where they lay. They had been taken by surprise: the mother had died first, the two girls afterwards, together in the same room. As he walked around it, he had wondered if the mother had brought the killer in with her.

'Is this what you would call a serial killer?'

'Motive is certainly obscure. At the moment.'

'Killing for the sake of killing, then?'

'Certainly I felt a hint of pleasure in it.'

Perhaps not in the Minden Street killings, but in the murder of Dr Murray, the careful way the heads had been laid out around her seemed as if the killer had savoured what he was doing.

If it was a he. Could be a woman.

But he thought there was some evidence of physical

strength. Dr Murray was a tall, strong woman, who apparently had not struggled. Also, one of the twins, Alice, he thought, had large bruises on her upper arms, as if big strong hands had gripped her hard.

There might just be a fingerprint to be culled there. Out of the bruise. Worth thinking about.

'The traffic light has changed,' said Stella gently. 'Safe to go.'

A bruise and a smell. Not much to work on, and certainly not the sort of information to lay before Phoebe Astley.

'Let's go for a drive,' said Coffin to Stella. 'So I can think.'

'You mean I'm not to talk?' Stella wound a scarf round her head.

'Now and then.' He gave her a friendly look but said nothing else. Stella closed her eyes. It was possible she slept, but she had the distinct impression they were across the river and driving round Blackheath, then down to Greenwich where she and Coffin had first met.

She put her hand on his wrist. 'I know where we are. And I know why: you are talking with ghosts.'

'Perhaps we shouldn't have left, Stella.'

'We didn't have a choice. Life picked us up and moved us on. It always does.' Then she said, 'And now it's dropped us back.'

'We'd better go home.'

'And don't say that home is always where I am . . . You can write better dialogue than that.'

Coffin laughed. 'Besides which, we would both have been homeless for about thirteen years when we were apart. Come on, I don't know what it is about St Luke's Tower with you in it, but I like it. I reckon it's as near home as you and I will ever have. We'd better get another cat. After all, we still have a dog.' Gus had been ill but had survived. As probably, Coffin felt, he always would do.

He turned the car and drove back to the Second City.

Phoebe, as ever, did not let any grass grow beneath her feet.

There was a message on the answerphone by the time they got back to St Luke's Tower, after their drive through the past and after Stella had cast a wistful look at her theatre complex, and Coffin had parked the car in the underground garage that he had had constructed, since life up above was dangerous for a Chief Commander's cars. One petrol bomb too many.

The message said that a car would be calling for him NOW to take him to 20 Nean Street, where Nat and her husband, Jason Broad, lived. Out of the shadow of her powerful cousin, she was always Nat or Natty. The change of name seemed to change her too. Or so Phoebe, who had known her briefly as a friend of a friend, thought.

Phoebe was driving the car herself. 'Want to be introduced, or want to be anonymous?' she asked as he settled into his seat.

'Anon would be easiest, but it's too late.'

There was a short thick-set figure, male he thought, it was just conjecture, sitting on the door step of no. 18, eating a stuffed bagel and making a messy job of it. He moved aside as they came past, giving them a bright, birdlike stare.

'Almost human,' observed Phoebe as she pushed past.

Coffin raised an eyebrow. 'Now, now.'

'Joke,' she said hastily. 'He's probably a mathematical genius busy working out the answer to quantum physics versus relativity.'

Coffin looked up and down the street, which he knew to be one of those streets in his bailiwick where a car could be stripped down of all, including the tyres, in a matter of minutes. It was now full night, so even more dangerous.

He went over to the seated figure, pushed two coins into his hand and said, 'Same again if the car is still there and in one piece when we get back.'

Sam nodded without a word and pocketed the money.

Natty and her husband were not the only people waiting for them. There was a third person, sitting on a hard, wooden chair, looking white and tired. Coffin and Phoebe were offered similar chairs. It was one of the bleakest rooms that Coffin had seen: plain white paint, cream walls, and a scattering of rugs on a polished wooden floor. Mugs of coffee stood on a round table.

'Dr Murray's husband,' said Phoebe. 'He just got here.'

He came forward, held out his hand. 'Dave Upping . . . Margaret's my wife.' Then he corrected himself. 'Was my wife. We were married all right, but she chose to keep her single name.' He was talking nervously and too quickly, as if he wanted to get the words out before they escaped him. 'I've been away. I work abroad a lot, I was in Paris, I'd taken the train . . . I can't believe she's gone. I want to see her.'

Coffin introduced them both. 'Chief Inspector Astley, and I am Chief Commander Coffin. I'm sorry if we've been slow.' Upping, on the other hand, had been very fast.

Dave nodded. 'You didn't have to introduce yourself. I've seen both of you around. I've even cut your hair once, sir, although you've forgotten.'

No answer for Coffin there, so he did not try to give one.

'I got the message on my mobile. I was already on the way home . . . I was near Waterloo, on the Eurostar. One of your chaps met me at the station and brought me back. Kind of him. Appreciate it. But I want to know, want to see her.'

'Glad we could do so,' said Coffin. And of course, it establishes that you were in Paris at the relevant time, and not over here killing your wife.

'I believe I will have to identify Margaret,' he said. 'Someone has got to.'

'Later,' said Coffin. 'Just a formality.'

'How was she killed? I know she was attacked, and I know where, in that bloody museum, but how?'

'She was shot. Probably by a handgun, but we don't have the weapon.'

Dave said in a dull voice. 'I knew it was murder, of course, not an accident.'

Coffin thought: It's most often husbands who kill wives.

You could buy an alibi, or hire a gunman. Check. Check the man, Phoebe. She caught his look.

'How was that?' Phoebe had been silent; now she spoke.

'Margaret had been worried. I thought perhaps she was ill or wondered if she was. She said no.'

'But she admitted to being worried?'

'She didn't deny it.'

'No clues?'

Dave shook his head.

Phoebe looked at Nat, who shook her head. 'I don't know. I was worried myself about her, but there was nothing I could put a finger on.'

'Right,' said Phoebe. 'Later on we will be taking statements from you.' She looked at Natty and Jason. 'From all of you. Just routine, something we have to do. To get places and people and times clear.' She gave one of her radiant, kind smiles that meant nothing. 'And, also, taking a look at Dr Murray's house.' Which we will search thoroughly and ruthlessly, just to see what we can find.

'It's my home too,' he said dully.

'Don't worry, we shall not make a mess.'

Thus laying out, whether he knew it or not, the pattern of the next twenty-four hours. You got these jobs done at once, or their validity drained away like water from a bowl with a hole in it.

People, witnesses, could be such tellers of untruths. Rooms, objects even, did not like it, but had to be caught quickly before time altered them, corrupted their first honesty.

Natasha stretched out a hand quickly. 'Don't worry, Dave. We'll be with you, won't we, Jason?'

'Every step of the way,' Jason said promptly.

'Stay here tonight with us. Don't go home until tomorrow.'

Dave smiled. 'Thanks. I'll be better off at home. On my own.'

Phoebe produced a small plastic bag in which rested the golden ring that had rolled from Margaret Murray's pocket. She held it up so they could all see.

'Do you recognize it?'

'No.' Dave stared at it. 'Looks like a wedding ring. Not Margaret's; she never wore one.'

Natasha looked it and shook her head.

'May not be important,' said Phoebe easily. 'We'll find out.'

The mobile phone rang in her pocket. 'Excuse me.' She disappeared into the hall.

She was soon back and gave a nod to the Chief Commander. He tried to read her expression but failed.

'Inspector Dover will be round with Sergeant Helen Ash to take your statements and to go over the house and so on. He will set up all the arrangements.'

Coffin gave her a small nod, which let her know they would be off for now.

When they were outside in the car, Coffin turned to her. 'Well?'

'You asked for the blood to be tested pronto, sir.'

'I did.'

'Good guess, sir. There was blood of two types: O and AB.'

'Both pretty common.'

'Margaret Murray was O.'

'So we are looking for an AB killer.'

Phoebe drove on in silence, there was a knot of traffic to get through. When she was clear, she said, 'The AB blood was loaded with morphine . . .'

'A user. I suppose that might make identification easier.'

Phoebe drove the length of the street before adding a further bleak comment.

'Yes, also HIV positive.'

Coffin absorbed this in silence, then, 'What about the trace of blood on the skull?'

'It's difficult to get a type from such a small trace, and one that has been in water, but he's trying . . . One thing though he did say and I dare say you've thought so yourself: that particular skull cannot have been in the water long else all the blood would have washed away.'

Phoebe thought she knew where the blood could have come from.

'Hospitals are the place for blood,' was what Stella said when he got home and told her.

The police investigators of the two sets of killings, those of Dr Murray and the women in Minden Street, had as yet no intimation that the Walkers Club, an occasion rather than a formal gathering, numbers variable with some hangers-on, and meeting in the local library, in the park and at the local supermarket, was later found to be intimately involved with the deaths.

The members had only one thing in common: childbirth. They had met at ante-natal and post-natal classes, agreeing that if there was a time when you needed friends it was when you had a baby. The children got older but the Walkers – they had all pushed prams, hadn't they? – stayed together.

4

Later on Friday. On to Saturday.

Stella repeated her observation as she handed him a drink. 'Hospitals are the places for blood.'

Coffin accepted the drink. 'I don't know about the hospital. It's likely the blood came from the killer.'

She could be very acute. 'Was there a weapon on the murder scene?'

'No. And yes, we saw the importance. If Dr Murray carried a weapon that inflicted enough damage to make her attacker bleed so much, then where is that weapon? Not on her, or by her, or underneath her.'

'Perhaps he . . . I say he, but of course . . .'

'It could have been she . . . yes, perhaps the killer took that weapon with him, along with his own.'

It was impossible, Coffin found, to avoid the masculine: he was convinced this killer was a man. But he had been wrong before.

'Be interesting to see that weapon . . . gun . . . if it hasn't been dropped in the river.'

'Don't keep reading my thoughts,' growled Coffin, but he did it affectionately. He was used to Stella's intuitive advances into his mind. 'Yes, we must find the weapon. It may have been used before.'

'In Minden Street?'

'Could be.'

'If it's the same killer, then what is the motive?'

Coffin shrugged. 'You tell me. Perhaps the killer is a seriously deranged person.'

'A loony.'

'There are more elegant ways of putting it, but yes. It's not an elegant world out there.'

'Hate, revenge, those are motives too,' said Stella.

'It's the tiny skulls that I don't like. There's a message to be read there, but I can't read it.'

'You've got a loony at work,' repeated Stella, chewing an olive. She saw her husband's expression. 'All right. I take that back. Not worthy of me. But I have had half a dinner, a long wait in the car, and a drive through the past . . . although I don't think we got there.'

'I did,' said Coffin in a low voice.

'And I think I have had too much to drink,' went on Stella.

'Not you, you're never drunk.'

Stella laughed. 'It's because I'm a performer. I can cover it up. Still, it's good sometimes to sit a bit loose to the world.'

'Is that what you are doing now?'

'Stops my thinking about all those sad babies. The primitive early ones, buried in the grave near your office, and all those lined up in the museum as teaching specimens . . . I think that's worse, truly.'

She was drunk, Coffin thought, and prepared to get weepy any moment. Not like his Stella. She never cried, except professionally.

He stood up. 'I'll make some coffee . . . I could do with some myself.'

Before brewing the coffee, he went up the winding staircase to the very top of the tower, where the workroom had been contrived for him. His study he would not call it, because what did he study there? But he did work there.

At the door, he hesitated; he could see that the answerphone had no message for him, nor was the fax spewing out a ribbon of paper.

Good. So far so good.

But there was something about his room. His work table had not been moved, he could still sit there looking out of the window across to the old churchyard, but he felt as though someone was looking at him.

He swung round. Someone was looking at him. Serious bronze eyes stared back. Bronze eyes in a bronze face.

It was a stylized bronze portrait bust with all the features and neck slightly elongated. Not unpleasing, but not natural either. The arms were folded across the chest, with the hands extended. The hands were very long and thin.

The bronze was on a black pedestal to the right of the door. All was normal in the rest of the room, his room, except for this bronze visitor. He gave a checking glance round the room. No other intruder.

'I hope you are a visitor,' he addressed it carefully. 'And not here to stay.'

As he walked past it, he saw that the creature possessed another arm; a third arm protruded from the right shoulder blade . . .

He closed the door carefully behind him.

He was tired, but he knew he would not sleep. Too many unpleasant images were floating around in his head.

The kitchen was clean, neat and empty. They had no animal present, the last incumbent, Gus, was still in the animal clinic, determined to come home. Coffin missed the friendly presence. He would have liked to have had a cat comfortably asleep in his basket. The basket was still there, but empty.

Coffin felt deeply depressed, especially when he discovered he was making tea instead of coffee and had to start again. He took particular care about arranging the china, the fine bone stuff that Stella liked (a long life in the police had accustomed Coffin to the thickest of china mugs), and getting out a few biscuits. Stella would not eat them; she was counting the calories again this season.

'What about getting a cat?' he asked Stella as he pushed into the sitting room with his tray.

She turned to look. 'Watch it, you've got a spot of coffee on your sleeve.'

Better than blood, he thought, as he dabbed at it. Come to think of it, if the killer had spilt all that blood, wouldn't he have it on his clothes too? And if so, why hadn't someone noticed?

Hospitals were places for blood, as Stella had observed. Perhaps he ought to be looking for a surgeon.

A mad one, according to Stella.

'It was water,' he said, rubbing at his sleeve. But that other spot on his trouser leg was coffee right enough; he hoped Stella would not notice. She abhorred spots on clothes, whereas any copper would tell you that they went with the job.

He knew he was at the stage in the case when, had he still been out in the field doing hard graft, he would have admitted to being in a muddle. From which, with hard work and co-operation from the rest of the team, a truth would emerge.

As a rule.

'I've been thinking, while you were making the coffee.'

'I thought you were asleep.'

'That too.' She drank some coffee. 'I did dream a bit, one of those short little dreams . . . And I thought: Not killing the babies, but kind of collecting them.'

She looked at him, wide-eyed. Just so might Mary Shelley have looked at Percy Bysshe as she read him passages from *Frankenstein*, with Byron listening.

It was quite an idea, Coffin thought.

'No, I don't think so, Stella. All the other infants were long dead, thousands of years, but forensics have now told us that the modern one is probably nearer a hundred, an easy task they said.' It looked as though it had been stolen from the museum and planted among the much older skulls.

'There's a rational element here, Stella. This killer is organized, I swear. He does it his way.'

He had read that there were two sorts of serial killers:

the organized and the disorganized. He thought he had an organized one here.

'A two-headed monster,' said Stella sleepily as she sipped her coffee. 'I'm going to try to get Peter Storey to give me his new play.'

'Is he writing one?' Storey was a golden name in the theatre.

'He's always writing one. All writers always have a play or a novel in the bottom drawer.'

Her husband was not paying her much attention, still caught up with his own thoughts about the killer. 'Maybe organized is not quite the right word,' mused Coffin. 'More just lucky.'

'If you say he is organized,' declared Stella with great loyalty, 'then he is. You always get it right.' She then took away some of the force of this statement, by saying, 'Whatever being organized for murder means. Do you mean he is paid?'

'I didn't mean that, but I might consider it.'

'Any news of Joan Lumsden?'

'None. Or if there is, then no one has told me.'

'Oh, you would be told.' Stella was incredulous at the idea that her husband could be kept in the dark.

Coffin shrugged. 'His mates would close ranks.'

Slowly Stella said, 'You can't mean they think he killed her . . . they would never protect him then.'

'No, but they might not help to drop him in it.'

Silence, he thought, was a great weapon.

'He's on leave, I suppose?'

Coffin nodded. 'Seems best. Anyway, he's not in any shape to work. Apparently.' There was a little chill in his voice, suggesting that he did not quite believe in Detective Constable Lumsden's ill health. He was under pressure, certainly.

'What about the blood in her car?' The story of the blood had figured a great deal in the press, so it was no secret. 'Is it hers?' Blood again, she thought, a lot of blood around at the moment.

Coffin shrugged. 'Not known. She isn't around to check, and many people have blood of her type. It is certainly not his.'

'And it is human blood?'

'A good guess, Stella – that question was raised since their dog is missing too – but, yes, it is human.'

He got up and started to move about the room. 'Dead or alive, I wish she'd turn up.'

One of the men who had worked with Lumsden had said that he thought Lumsden missed the dog as much as his wife. This joke (question mark here) had been passed on to Coffin. It showed how Lumsden was rated by his colleagues. You didn't make that sort of joke about someone you liked and respected.

He'd known a copper like that himself in his youth; he could still remember his name, Len Daley. A man who had worked by the rule, doing his job but without imagination. He was probably a high-ranking officer by now, but he had never come Coffin's way, so it was guesswork.

'Could be dead,' he said aloud.

Stella waited to hear if he amplified this statement, then asked, 'Who is dead?'

Coffin stared at her but he did not speak; he was far away.

'Who are you talking to?'

He gave himself a shake. 'To myself. A ghost walking.' Then he laughed. Ridiculous to think of Daley as a ghost when he was probably alive, prosperous and master of a household. If he had a household, then he would certainly be master of it; that was his style.

'Am I master in this household?' he said aloud to Stella.

She looked surprised. 'Now what are you talking about? First ghosts, and now masters of households . . . Let me tell you, no one talks in those terms now.'

'Some of them still think it,' said Coffin humbly. 'And I only asked.'

'Well, the answer is that you are not.'

'I thought I wasn't. I knew you'd know.'

Stella gave him a suspicious look.

'Just so I know: who is?'

'Of course there isn't one. We don't live like that.'

'Glad to know it. So who rearranged my workroom?'

Stella said that she supposed she had. And did it matter?

'Not in itself, but there is the stranger in the corner. If it is a stranger; looks familiar to me.'

'You know who it is?' Stella was relieved. This was going to be easier than she had feared . . . Letty, Letty, what have you done to me? 'You recognized the face?'

'I didn't think it was Julius Caesar.'

'It's from your sister, Letty, it's a surprise.'

'It was that all right.'

'It's by Elijah Jones, he's a coming man, Letty thinks a lot of him. He's a bit quirky, of course.'

'He's certainly that.'

'You mean the third arm?' said Stella nervously. 'You may not have had a chance to see, but there's another eye at the back of your head . . . It symbolizes what you are: someone who sees round corners and solves problems.'

Letty Bingham was Coffin's much younger half-sister; she had reappeared in his life just at the time when, finding his mother's diary, he had concluded that, although long vanished, Mother might still be alive. Letty had grown up in the States, and was now a lawyer and a banker and rich. At intervals she descended upon the Second City to see her half-brother, sometimes with a new husband, sometimes newly divorced. Recently she had given up what she called 'the marrying game'. Needless to say, she and Stella liked each other.

'He's getting famous and your bust will be very valuable in time,' said Stella.

'So I'm an investment now, am I?' grumbled Coffin. 'Well, the thing is in my way. Move it, please.'

Nervously Stella said she thought she was hungry. 'We didn't eat much. Would you like some soup?'

She couldn't make soup, but she was good at opening tins, and these days the best soups came in cardboard containers that you kept in the fridge. She investigated and found none. Oh well, it would have to be hunger and bed.

She knew how to make bed attractive.

To her surprise, Coffin found the alternative attractive. He had been half asleep; now he woke up, pointing out that it was just as well there wasn't a dog to take for a walk before going to bed.

'You're better than tomato soup,' he said at one point, 'but you smell of vanilla.'

'It's my new scent.'

'What a shame, I thought you might be a new biscuit, edible of course. Vanilla cream . . . That third arm might have its uses now,' he observed a little later on. 'Not to mention various other bits of the anatomy.'

Stella laughed.

There was no more conversation for a bit, only what Coffin later called a congress of the spirit.

Later still he said sleepily, 'You will hide the bronze, won't you? Don't want to live with an elongated version of myself.'

'I believe Letty will want to borrow it for an exhibition she is mounting in London.'

'As long as my name is not on it.' He was almost asleep.

Stella did not tell him that his name and rank were inscribed on the back of the bronze head under the third eye.

Chief Inspector Phoebe Astley was not sleeping well. The sex games she played with her friend Jo were just that, games, but she was beginning to be aware that they could fire into something more serious. The trouble was that she wanted a child, but she didn't want a husband. Well, there were ways round that problem, and Jo knew them. She was a doctor, but her price would be a relationship with Phoebe.

You ought to want a husband, she told herself, or anyone

who would make a male partner, or just think of offspring from an anonymous source. Of course, it didn't have to be anonymous, but it had to be said there were no eager applicants around at the moment.

Her friendship with the Chief Commander, going back some years, frightened a lot of colleagues away.

She turned over in bed, then reached out for a glass of water. Would the Chief Commander be prepared to make a helpful donation? Joke.

She drank some more water. What a terrifying child it would be, with her genes and his.

She lay back on her pillow, drifting towards sleep. She knew that she would never forget the infant skulls, first the little Neanderthal heads and then the collection in the medical museum. It was hard to know which was the most poignant.

'I heard someone say that Neanderthals could not speak, they had no language. It's thought they could make grunting noises but that their throats, tongues also, were the wrong shape for speech.'

It made it worse to Phoebe that those long dead little creatures had had no names.

An evolutionary change altered the shape of our throats and mouth, one which moved the tongue forward and shortened the jaw. Thus modern man learned to speak, and speaking pushed the Neanderthals into oblivion. They might, in their way, have been loving family creatures, but since they could not say so, they were lost.

On the other hand, Phoebe remembered, they might have made a sacrificial offering of the infants. So they had gods whom they could not name but who demanded a tribute.

As she relaxed into sleep, she drew up a list of what she should do in the morning, as she always did.

Read the interview with the cousin Natasha and her husband, Jason, that Sergeant Helen Ash had undertaken. Helen was good at these sensitive first interviews, but she herself would conduct another questioning. Inspector Dover would be talking to the husband, Dave. Once again, Phoebe would talk to him.

She would also interview the SOCO, studying his photographs and diagrams . . .

Infant skulls again . . . She hoped he would be schematic about this, and not seek likenesses. She didn't want to see infant faces staring back at her.

Post-mortem on Dr Murray with the Chief Commander. Nice of him to come, if he did.

She drifted into sleep.

Sergeant Ash was gentle with Natty and Jason. She could see they were both in shock.

'I would like to have seen my cousin . . . if it is her, it might have been someone else.'

'Had you seen her before she was killed? In the evening, I mean?'

Natty shook her head. 'No, she was at her own home, waiting for her husband, they were going out to dinner when he got back, I think.'

She dealt with Dave Upping even more tactfully. He repeated the story of being in Paris, providing the address: François, Rue du Bac. 'You can check.'

Ash smiled and nodded. So we will, she told herself, you can count on that. 'I expect the Chief Inspector will want to speak to you tomorrow, sir.'

When Ash had gone, Dave accepted a strong drink of whisky and allowed himself to be shepherded to bed. 'I won't sleep.'

'No,' said Natty. 'I won't either, but get some rest. It's going to be a tough time.'

She looked at her husband. 'It's going to be tough for us too. I'm frightened.'

He put his arm round her. 'We'll come through.'

Phoebe Astley was in the large room set aside as the Murder Room from early the next morning. Since it was a large room it was also being used by the other team she belonged to that was working on the Minden Street murders. She was now reading the transcript of Inspector Ash's interviews. Ash had done a good job, but it was only a beginning. Phoebe would question them each herself.

'Not much to be learned from what Ash has got as yet,' she thought, as she put the files of reports aside. After some consideration she picked up the file on the Minden Street killings. Inspector Dover and his deputy had put this and various artefacts together on a table; next to it, on a larger table, lay the women's bloodstained clothes, together with a few personal possessions.

Clothes after forensic examination, neatly folded and packaged in plastic bags, some blood showing.

Shoes, handbags. Three handbags, one for each woman. These too were wrapped in plastic. Beside them, but in separate plastic covers, were lipsticks, powder compacts and several opened letters. The letters had been neatly arranged in a pile.

Other objects had been removed from the house for forensic examination. Cups, glasses and knives and forks. There was one photograph in a silver frame. The face, that of a man, seemed familiar. 'With love from Jack' was scrawled across the bottom of the picture. That made it Black Jack Jackson, ten years younger.

Reluctantly Phoebe was accepting that he was still the most likely killer of his sisters and his mother.

She turned to the file of notes that Dover and Co. had left . . . not Dover she suspected; he had delegated that task.

Very little had been made of the photograph, except for identifying it and adding the note that he had been interviewed.

Then there was a list of people and addresses named in the letters with the note 'Not yet interviewed'.

Josie Aspinall.

Geoff Gish.

Mrs Lirie at the fish shop.

Dr Murray.

That name meant something to Phoebe, as she knew it would to Coffin. Interested to see what more she could find out, she turned to the letters.

There was nothing she could find that appertained to Dr Murray other than her name on an envelope.

Was the envelope to her or from her or just a note of her name? Impossible to tell, but it made a link between the two murders. Whoever had killed the other victims maybe had Dr Murray in mind.

It was still very early morning, but she was so anxious to get in touch that she picked up the telephone. The Chief Commander had better be an early riser. In the old days he had been.

Stella answered the telephone. 'Good morning, Phoebe.'

'Can I speak to the Chief Commander?'

'He's still asleep.' Then Stella added thoughtfully, 'But I can wake him up.'

'No need,' called a voice. 'I'm awake. Any coffee going?' He walked over to the telephone. 'That you, Phoebe?'

'Yes. How did you know?'

'No one but you would call at this hour of the morning. And it's the Minden Street murders, isn't it?'

'Yes.'

'You've found a connection with Dr Murray? You've found the weapon?'

'No, but there is an envelope with her name on it. The writing has not yet been identified.'

'Get hold of Jack Jackson. It may be his. Get hold of him, anyway.'

Jack had taken himself off, but the police were looking.

'He was questioned when the three bodies were found. Inspector Dover talked to him.'

'Bring him in again. But handle him quietly.'

'Yes, right,' said Phoebe. She hesitated before reminding him that he had felt sure Black Jack was not a killer. 'Are you suggesting he also killed Dr Murray?' She was crossing her fingers.

'I know what I said about him not being killer material. I still think that's the case, but I would like to see him faced with a few questions. I want to question him.'

'What about the PM on Dr Murray?'

'See if you can get that rearranged. Who's down to do it?'

Phoebe consulted her notes. 'Dr Everle . . . he's easy, he won't mind.' Probably had a stack of bodies lined up. There had been a bad coach crash the day before and a couple of suicides in the river.

'Right.'

Jack was already out in the streets, walking. Early morning or late night were all one to him; this was when he liked to walk. Everyone has their habits and this was his, well known to his associates and the police.

5

Saturday, very early.

Jack Jackson, revelling for the moment in his nickname
Black Jack, strolled through the streets of the Second City.
He had just had a spat with Mimsie Marker, who was tidying
her stall before setting up the papers for the early-morning
travellers. It was always hard to know when Mimsie slept.
A quarrel with Mimsie was one of his treats, setting him up
for the day, and he suspected that Mimsie felt the same: they
both enjoyed a rousing disagreement. They had known each
other since childhood, when they had attended the same
school and sat side by side on a double bench, pushing at each
other and squabbling. Honours were about equal in those
battles, and fondly remembered, but their ways had parted as
they grew up, except when they met at Mimsie's paper stall.

While not offering him any sympathy for the deaths of the
women in Minden Street (it was always hard to know what
to say to Jack that was not a well-turned insult or a joke),
she was one of those who knew he was no killer.

She gave his departing back a wave while she sold the next
customer a paper and a sandwich. As she did so, she totted
up the extra profits that were coming her way since she had
added soft drinks and sandwiches to the stall.

'No,' she said to the customer. 'That was not the man
whose mother and sisters had been murdered.'

The customer leaned forward to tap Mimsie's arm. 'You
want your eyes tested, Mimsie Marker, or to get counselling,

71

because you've lost it. That was Black Jack. I think I'll follow him.' And the customer passed on, neglecting to pay for the sandwich so that Mimsie ground her teeth in anger.

Jack Jackson turned into the narrow alley, officially Watermen's Row but known locally as Piss Passage, which led to the riverside near where he lived. When he moved out of the Minden Street establishment (by mutual consent), he had bought a loft conversion above an old factory. To his surprise, another small factory had moved in so that there were now women busy sewing away at T-shirts while he lived in his large empty space above. He liked it rather than otherwise; he could hear the machines going and the women laughing and talking. Not a word of English, but who minded?

He would miss what he called 'the Minden Street gang', because in his own way he had loved them. Quarrel yes, but retain a liking and respect, oh yes.

He knew he was top of the list of suspects. Probably the only suspect. If the police could have found any evidence or even a motive that pointed at him, then he would have been inside, but they had nothing. Fair enough, since he had not killed his mother and sisters.

Nor did he have any idea who had done it. He had just one thing his mother had said to him in the week before the murder.

'Know what, I feel worried. I feel like there's a hand on my neck.'

'Oh go on, Mum. Not like you.'

'Do you know that man Coffin?'

'I know Coffin,' he had said in a level voice.

'I think I'll have a talk with him.'

'You do that, Mum.'

But she had died before she could. 'I'll have that talk with Coffin,' he said to himself. 'I can do that for her.'

He heard the soft shuffle of feet, moving quietly. He was a loud mover himself. He swung round.

'Hello.' He was surprised. He was opening his mouth to say something else when the bullet sliced into his neck.

A voice spoke quietly into his ear. 'Sorry you didn't get done with the others. I would have done you with them, if you had been there. Not that you were paid for, you understand; I did you for free.'

Jack slid to the ground, sightless and speechless. 'I will not die,' he said to himself. 'I will not die.'

But he had the terrible feeling that this was him dying.

'No Christmas for me,' he said on a dying breath. 'Why me? Why do I have to die?'

6

Saturday, but no weekend.

Coffin had known even before he woke up, summoned back to life by Phoebe's telephone call, that it was going to be a difficult day. He would go to the PM on Dr Murray as promised.

Stella too knew it was not going to be one of those easy days. She had rolled over on her pillow and without opening her eyes asked him what he had been muttering about in the night.

'I don't know. What did I say?'

Stella opened her eyes. 'Well, you didn't say: Darling Stella, what a perfect wife you are and how heavenly to have you by my side.'

It was at this point that she had got up, put on her favourite pink silk dressing gown, and gone to make the coffee. She took a sneaking pleasure in being well dressed when speaking to Phoebe, wearing something Phoebe could not afford nor would have chosen if she could. Phoebe could be an intimidating person when she chose, so Stella liked to have her own weapons ready.

Stella served the coffee in her own special china, bought when she had been acting in a play about an aristocratic comedy of the eighteenth century called *The King and Lady Bunbury*.

'I don't know if I muttered last night, but I couldn't sleep well,' said Coffin as he accepted the cup.

'It shows,' said Stella dispassionately. 'You're getting too old to go without your sleep.'

'Five o'clock in the morning, or is it later?'

'Six,' said Stella. 'Nearly.' A bit of a lie; it was nearer five.

'Six o'clock, you haven't slept well and you are dragged out of bed with a piece of information that might or might not be important in a murder case. How would you look?' He drained the cup. 'And I've got the feeling that there's worse to come.'

'Do you think Phoebe rang that early on purpose?'

'Why should she do that?'

Stella shrugged. Well, who knows? the shrug said.

Even as she spoke, the telephone rang again. 'Your turn,' she said to Coffin.

'Hello.'

She saw him frown. 'Go on,' he said.

She could hear Phoebe's voice, easy to recognize her tones, but this time her voice was high, shrill, not like her usual voice at all.

'Wait, wait, hold your breath. Don't start being too clever, Phoebe.'

Phoebe said something out of which Stella picked the word 'dead'.

'Dead or not dead . . . I can't get the hang of this on the telephone . . . Come across and talk here. Stella will give you some coffee.' He looked towards Stella who nodded.

'Who's dead?'

'Black Jack . . . someone's put a bullet through his throat. He may not be dead. His heart stopped but the doctors are working on it.'

'Phoebe sounded upset.'

'Yes, she is. Dead's dead to her.'

'I mean, more than you would expect. Professionally,' she added, as Coffin seemed not prepared to say anything.

'Black Jack's an attractive man,' he said finally. 'Are you getting the coffee for Phoebe?'

'So?'

'I think they had a relationship once,' said Coffin reluctantly. 'I never enquired.'

'She's a woman of surprises. I always knew she put it about a bit, but really . . .' Stella was trying to sound both shocked and surprised when she was neither. 'And I don't believe you never asked questions.'

'Well, only in the way of work, and not directly to her.'

Stella nodded. It would make a good play, this would. 'I'll get dressed.'

'You look lovely as you are.'

'I know. That's why. It's not fair on Phoebe.'

She took her time dressing, a long grey wool and silk skirt with a cashmere sweater. Gold earrings. Then she made some more coffee, but still no sign of CI Astley.

'She's in no hurry,' she said, sailing in with a tray of hot, fresh coffee and the best china.

'I thought I heard the car,' said Coffin looking out of the window. 'Yes, she's here, but I can't see what she's doing.'

Stella joined him. 'She's crouched over something. I hope it's not another body. Not in our back yard.'

The large, elegantly paved square between the church tower and the new parts of the theatre was no one's back yard.

Coffin moved away from the window. 'Whatever it is, she's bringing it to our front door.'

It must be a head, thought Stella; she couldn't carry a body. She hurried down the curving staircase to where Phoebe was ringing the bell.

Phoebe was there, cradling in her arm a small, emaciated young cat, hardly more than a kitten.

'I found it outside. It's been abandoned, I think it's starving. Dehydrated too.'

Coffin stroked the tabby head with a gentle forefinger, and the little creature looked back with no expression in its yellow eyes.

'We'd better get some water down it and then some food. Got any fish, Stella?'

'In a tin,' she said. Stella had only ever seen large, plump healthy animals, never one like this bedraggled little specimen. Death, she thought, might be its next encounter.

'We will try to get it to eat a little, but we must get the vet to it . . . He probably ought to take it away so it can be nursed properly, unless the shock of moving it kills it. But I think it's past that, we must just try.' All the time he was gently stroking it.

Stella had a busy day ahead but it did not include a string of murders and an overwrought CI Astley. Life was to be sought rather than death for a tabby stray as much as anyone else. 'I'll organize it,' she said.

'So what about Black Jack?' asked Coffin over the kitten's head.

'His throat was hit; he must have swung round and got shot there . . . He was found by the next person down Piss Passage . . . when the ambulance got there his heart had stopped.'

'Dead,' said Coffin.

'Pre-dead. It's a new state. Get to you fast enough and they can bring you back.'

'And the medics did?'

'Yes, they're mighty clever, but he might stop breathing again any minute, or he might be brain-damaged. He lost a lot of blood. I don't know how he'd feel about that. He might think they'd been too clever.'

'I expect he'd rather be alive than dead,' said Coffin, still stroking the cat. 'And you think the attacker was the one who did for his mother and his sisters?'

'At the moment it's the only idea I have.'

'Evidence?'

'Nothing as yet, except the nature of the wound in the neck. The same sort of weapon. But that's only guessing.'

Good guesses count for a hell of a lot, as Coffin knew well.

'And Dr Murray?'

'Another one done by the same killer.'

'Hm.' Coffin stopped stroking the cat, to whom Stella was now administering spoonfuls of milk and water.

'Kill or cure,' she said. She gathered up the little animal. 'I'll take over now; the vet said he'd be here within twenty minutes. First call of the day.'

'Let me know how it goes,' said Phoebe.

'Right,' said Stella.

Coffin watched her walk away with the cat. Darling Stella, she always came through when it counted. If the kitten lived, and she would see it did, then it would be with them for the rest of its life.

He swung round to Phoebe.

'No infant skulls around this one's head?'

'Not this time.'

'None around in Minden Street either.'

'Mrs Janey Jackson was a maternity nurse, though.'

Coffin looked up in surprise. 'Was she? I didn't know that.'

Phoebe had herself under control by now. 'If Jack dies, it might be an idea to have the post-mortem on him and Dr Murray one after the other.'

'Would Dr Everle take that?'

George Everle was Professor Dennis Garden's senior assistant. Garden was so eminent and famous that he was absent a good deal on what he called 'important university business'. He had a very handsome set of rooms in the shining, gleaming new department that had been built under his magic. Everyone agreed that Professor Garden had magic.

'Oh nothing worries Everle . . . just doesn't get through; if you see as many bodies as he does, then one more doesn't matter.' Of course, she didn't go to many PMs herself these days, nor did the Chief Commander (when had been the last?), so the simultaneous arrival of both of them might cause Everle to raise an eyebrow. If he looked at them at all.

As she left, Phoebe said to Coffin, 'By the way, do tell Stella to watch the scraps of paper with important notes on that she drops. I picked this up in the hospital and it has a telephone number on it. And I think there might have been others.'

'I'll tell her,' said Coffin absently. He was thinking about Black Jack. Dead or alive?

But Black Jack was not dead. He was hardly alive, not conscious, and the prognosis was not good, but dead he was not.

Coffin got on with routine work, receiving at intervals bulletins about Black Jack from the hospital and the kitten from Stella.

Stella reported that the vet thought the kitten would do well now it was in care; he was giving it a special food. Stella added that it was female, had been badly treated, bruised, but it was not in kitten. She had told the vet that she would be giving it a home, but would be having it neutered.

Coffin was mildly surprised because she had tolerated rather than loved the various animals he had brought with him into their lives. Except Gus, the dog; she loved Gus. 'You don't mind, do you?'

'No, Stella, be nice to have a cat again. My familiar.'

'I feel guilty, you see. I heard a cat crying, several times, and I never did anything. It might have died if Phoebe hadn't brought it in.'

'No need to feel guilty. Or not on your own. I could have heard the cat too and done something.'

'Oh you had murders and such on your mind . . . I expect in the end she will be more your cat than mine.'

'I give you my share,' said Coffin generously.

'Any news of Jack?'

'He's not dead. Not quite alive, either.'

'He was shot?'

'Yes, in the neck. Only the fact that he was wearing a coat with a collar up protected him . . . deflected the bullet a bit, so the surgeons say. They've got the bullet out.' Phoebe's outfit had wanted the bullet to see if it made a match with the bullets in the other killings.

He worked on, dictating a report to one of his secretaries, and taking a phone call.

'Charley Fisher here, sir.'

Inspector Fisher had taken over from Sergeant Drury and was handling the delicate matter of the missing Mrs Lumsden.

'Just to say, sir, that there has come a postcard from Mrs Lumsden. Sent to her mother. Picture postcard of Teignmouth, postmarked South Devon. Teignmouth is in Devon.'

'I know that,' said Coffin irritably. 'What does it say?'

'It says her mother is not to worry, she is well.'

'Does she say why she went off?'

'No, just that she is in hiding.'

'In hiding? From whom?'

An almost audible shrug came over the telephone wire. 'From her husband, I take it, sir.'

'Is it a joke? Is it genuine?'

'The mother thinks it is her daughter's writing, but she isn't sure. And she has no idea what is meant by being in hiding.'

Into the silence, Fisher said, as reproachfully as he dared, 'You did say you wanted to be kept in touch with any development, sir.'

'So what do you think? Is the card genuine?'

'The postmark is genuine. Last week. Took the mother that long to let us see it. But the card, well, it's an old one.'

Coffin was silent again. He should keep out of this, he was getting involved in too many cases that he ought to leave to the investigating teams. God knows, he had enough problems to deal with.

'You don't believe it,' he said suddenly.

'No, sir. Fishy.'

So that was it, for the moment. Arthur Lumsden was still in trouble, and so, by transference was the Second City Police. No one wanted an officer who had done in his wife. It was the last thing to cheer up an already anxious Chief Commander. Especially one who no longer felt he had the back-up of his surrounding office staff.

There had been a lot of changes in his office lately. The

secretaries that he had relied on had departed to promotion or maternity; he would always welcome them back if they fancied it, but meanwhile he had to take on fresh bodies.

Stella had told him that he depended too much on women, so now in addition to Paul Masters he had Sergeant Roger Adams (he liked to be called Rog, although not by the Chief Commander) and Sergeant Anthony Davies, a highly efficient young man with whom he was not yet on easy terms, while respecting his skills. Rumour had reached Coffin that Sergeant Davies was considering becoming Antonia Davies. Coffin had nothing against this; in fact, it took him back to his early days as a young constable still in uniform on the beat, when he had met his sergeant, a sturdy well-built figure of a man, on the tube going towards Piccadilly wearing a velvet skirt, an organza blouse with frills and a blond wig. He had been carrying a small white handbag on a hot summer day. In those days, a pub behind Fortnum's called the Flower of the Forest had been a chosen venue if you were looking for that sort of activity.

No words had been exchanged, no recognition admitted, none claimed. After all, the man was off duty.

Stella had laughed when he told her the story and asked what had happened to the man. Coffin had admitted that he had become Chief Constable – after all, he was a Scot – in a Scottish force. Presumably wearing a kilt.

He had not told her about Anthony/Antonia, and hoped the story was wrong.

Now he finished reading the report on Crime in the Inner City, initialled it and set out to to meet CI Astley.

You could walk from Coffin's office through gardens to the quiet building that housed the post-mortem suite, passing as you did so the hospital in which Black Jack now lay.

Coffin debated going in to the hospital to see how the man was doing. He had the sort of sneaking liking for Black Jack that he had had long ago for his sergeant in skirts.

The hospital building dated back to the beginning of the twentieth century, but it had recently had a wash and brush-up. Everything that could be repainted had been repainted. The whole building had been rewired and bits of smart, new equipment installed. But somehow it smelt the same.

Coffin knew enough about how things went to know that Jack Jackson was being nursed in high security, one constable outside the room and another by the bed. If Jack came back to life, he was a valuable witness.

Coffin knew where this room would be, third floor, but he checked at the central desk first. Yes, said the pretty young woman by the computer, he had it right. She looked at him with interest.

He made his own way up in the lift. The man sitting on the chair outside Jack's room was looking bored, but he knew Coffin and decided to jump up and look alert.

Coffin nodded at him, then went into the room. Jack lay in the bed, tethered to it by tubes and a machine with a flashing red light. He had seen it all before. He had never seen Black Jack look like this though: white and shrunken, yet with his face oddly puffy. His eyes seemed to be submerged in swollen flesh.

What thoughts are you having, Jack, if you are thinking at all?

He turned to the constable who had been sitting by the door. 'Has he said anything?' Coffin looked at him. 'Denton, isn't it?'

'Yes, sir . . . No, he hasn't spoken. Muttered a bit, just sounds and grunts, nothing you could make anything of.'

A nurse appeared through the door, a tall thin girl with spectacles and bright red hair. She gave Coffin a disapproving look. 'It's the Chief Commander? Would you like to see the doctor? I can get Dr Peters.'

Coffin refused this offer. From what he knew of hospitals, he guessed that a busy young doctor would not want to add a visit from the Chief Commander to his day. In any case there was little to say about Black Jack, whose hold on life seemed tenuous. The only thing in his favour that Coffin knew from experience was that you could not trust him to go either way. Unpredictable was what he was.

A trolley escorted by a nurse and pushed past him by a man in a pale blue tunic went down the corridor. The occupant of the trolley had closed eyes. Coffin hoped he was still alive. As they passed, the nurse gently drew the sheet over the patient's face.

The trio got to the row of lifts well before Coffin, who decided to use the stairs. There seemed less morbidity there.

Three flights to the ground floor, as he knew well. He was not alone: on every floor down he passed nurses and the hurrying figures of doctors who, he was interested to see, no longer wore the white coats as seen in films and soap operas. Time moves on.

Each floor was noisier and livelier than the last. Clearly if you were about to die, you went up to the top floor to be quiet about it.

He would probably be transported up there himself one of these days, hopefully to come down again. There were plenty ready to take a poke at him. Almost every week letters breathing hate and threats arrived at his office. Stella knew about them in general but not in particular, unless they seemed important. Nothing at the moment as far as he knew, although it was always his belief that the worst threat came without a signed warning.

Joe and his team, Sam and Matilda, saw him through the glass door on the ground floor.

'There he goes,' said Joe. 'Coffin.'

'Sort of good-looking in his way,' ventured Matilda, who was an expert in masculine good looks. 'Attractive. Don't you think so, Sam?'

'Oh, I suppose so.'

'You know what,' said Joe. 'I reckon he's the sort of chap who grew into his face. You have to have stamina to do that. It's a long-lived face,' he ended thoughtfully, leaning on the large vacuum cleaner that was his power symbol. Joe fancied himself as an expert on physiognomy.

Sam kept quiet, but he judged himself an expert in faces; he wanted to remind Joe that no one lived for ever.

No one had a sharper sense of the ease and unexpectedness of death than Coffin. His work forced it upon him. In the old days, he had gone to many a post-mortem as the senior detective in charge of a murder investigation.

Phoebe Astley was waiting for him. 'He's just started. We can go in. He's talking a bit, so it's not one of his silent days.'

'Oh,' Coffin nodded. 'Good.'

'Seems he knew Dr Murray. She used to come to talk to him sometimes about skeletal structures. He knows the husband too. Not sure how. Not over hair, I shouldn't think.'

Coffin reminisced as they walked in and the familiar odour of disinfectant and dead bodies reached him. It was interesting, he thought, how this smell, which had been banished when the new buildings first came into use, had now come back. 'He doesn't mind doing the PM? He could have got someone else.'

'No, quite matter of fact about it. He wants her killer caught, though, so he shows that much emotion.'

Coffin felt oddly glad about that: he did not want Dr Murray to be cut up too coldly. Professionally, yes, but with some heart.

It was soon done. Everle was a quick worker, aided by an efficient assistant, a young woman he was training.

He came over to them when he had removed his gloves and gown.

'She was shot in the back of the neck. The gun was 9mm; the bullet, had, of course, been removed already for forensics to work. Just the one shot. She died quickly, from massive blood loss. You will get the full report, of course.

'And, yes, in case you were going to ask: similar method of killing as Janey Jackson and her daughters.'

On the way out, Coffin said, 'We might have to add Jack Jackson to that list. He had a gunshot wound in the neck from the same type of gun.'

'I went in to see him,' Phoebe said in a carefully neutral voice.

'I thought you would. I went myself.'

'I don't think he'll pull through.' Her voice was even more carefully expressionless.

'He might.'

She really cares for that chap, he thought. That was the trouble with Black Jack; he was likeable. Unreliable but loveable. Damn him.

He had always been careful not to dig too deep into Phoebe's complicated emotional life, partly out of respect for her privacy, but as much for fear of being dragged into it, as he had been once, years ago. They had worked together often in the past, and it was the Chief Commander who had persuaded her to leave Birmingham to join his Force. They had had differences of opinion here and there, but he hoped she had never regretted the move.

She was a good detective and a loyal friend. Hang on to that thought.

Behind him, Phoebe said, 'Look who's there.'

In a car outside, Natasha and her husband Jason and Margaret Murray's husband Dave sat together, watching.

They knew what had been going on inside.

'I expect he wonders how we knew the hour and the day,' said Natty. In fact she worked three days a week at the medical library, and she knew and was known by most of the staff, from cleaners like Joe and Sam to the Chief Librarian himself.

She had not wanted to come.

'I needed to be here,' said Dave.

'Sure,' said Jason. 'We understood, didn't we, Natty?' He wound down the car window and nodded to Coffin.

'We don't have to speak to the police,' said Natasha. 'Not now, not at this minute. It's private.'

Coffin walked over.

'We don't have to introduce ourselves, do we?' Natasha was aggressive. 'And we know why you are here. Do the police always attend?'

'Usually,' said Coffin mildly.

'But not the big boss himself.'

'Pipe down, Natty,' said Dave. 'She's upset, Mr Coffin. We all are, but we wanted to come . . . well, I did. It's a part of mourning.'

'I understand.'

'Well, maybe. I reckon you have to have it happen to you in your own body. You were there in the way of business.' He was not so friendly as he had seemed at first.

Coffin did not answer.

'So, what was the verdict? Or do we have to wait for the inquest? There will be an inquest?' Definitely not friendly now.

'There will be an inquest,' agreed Coffin. Then he stopped.

'Of course,' said Phoebe from behind. 'Dr Murray died from a gunshot wound from a 9mm revolver.'

'Just one?'

'Yes,' said Phoebe. 'I'm sorry.'

'Didn't take much really, did it?' said Dave. 'Just one little shot and she was a goner.'

'We'll get the killer,' said Phoebe.

Dave wound up the window, put the car into gear, and drove off.

'Thanks for taking over,' said Coffin to Phoebe.

'I was afraid you were going to say we had no idea who the killer was and might never find him,' said Phoebe.

'I was terrified myself I would do just that.'

Coffin put Phoebe in her car and walked back to his office the same way he had come.

If he took a pace or two to the right, he would come to the place where the pool of infant heads had been found. If he looked hard he could see the roof of the house in Minden Street where Janey Jackson and her two daughters had died.

And on his left was the university block where Dr Murray had been shot.

Murder all around him, but what he could not see were any answers.

The murder of Dr Murray had to be linked to the murders of the Jackson family. Why it was necessary or desirable or good sport to kill Black Jack as well, Coffin could not decide.

He remembered the collection of infant skulls arranged around Dr Murray, as if in imitation of those found earlier.

There was the blood all around her, not all hers.

Blood and bones, that was what this case was all about.

On impulse, he walked round to the excavation where the infant Neanderthal skulls had rested. The water had drained away from the pit, which was now dry and neat. Two workmen were busy arranging a plastic covering. One man was tall and very thin, the other short and square.

'All tidied away, sir,' said the tall one. 'The vicar came along and said a prayer over them. Couldn't stop him.'

'Perhaps he was right,' said the short man.

'They'd been dead a long while. Too late to do them much good, I reckon, Jigger.'

'No,' said Jigger. 'You don't know about time, do you, sir? It may go round in a kind of circle so that it was always today for those little kids.'

Coffin accepted this without smiling, not sure where to put his feet in this philosophical mud. Vague memories of J.B. Priestley's three time plays, which Stella had produced and starred in, rose in his mind. 'Could be, I suppose.' It certainly was not a day he wanted repeated. Come to think of it, he wasn't sure he wanted life repeated at all.

'Don't think I want to be stuck here with you for ever,' said the tall man.

'We wouldn't know. Always a fresh moment in time to us, Pete, no matter how many times we went round.'

'See what I have to put up with, sir?' complained Pete.

*   *   *

Back in his office, Coffin called Phoebe Astley. 'What's become of the infant skulls?'

'Being looked after at the university. It seems they are of great archaeological importance.'

'And the other, newer skull?'

'That's different. Forensics still have it.'

'I see.'

No you don't, thought Phoebe, I can tell it in your voice. You're cross.

Coffin was not cross, but he was puzzled and depressed.

'What about the blood found with Dr Murray?'

'The blood that was not hers?'

'Yes.'

'Well, there we might have something . . . The hospital has an HIV clinic, a check is being made on the blood groups of any that matches the blood . . . When we get them, then we can interview all the names.'

He thought about it. 'What happens to blood? It doesn't just float around loose.'

'I asked about that, of course. If there is any quantity of blood, it is bottled. Sometimes it is washed and liquid is added, and it is used if a transfusion to that patient is necessary.'

'The blood is important,' said Coffin slowly.

Phoebe made a grunting assent.

'How do you rate it? Are you and your team coming to think of it as a serial killer at work?' Who might never be caught? He did not say this aloud, but it was there in his voice.

'It's coming that way,' admitted Phoebe.

7

Saturday still, and on to Monday.

Stella was waiting for him, and the little cat was on a cushion in a small basket. It looked new.

'I bought them for her,' said Stella proudly. 'The vet said I had a natural touch with her. He's one of my fans.'

'I bet.'

'Comes to everything I perform in.'

Coffin looked at the very pretty and, he had to say, expensive-looking basket and cushion. 'Did you buy the basket from him?'

'No, of course not, but he told me where to go in the covered market. An animal charity has a stall there; the profits, or some of them, go to the charity.'

The kitten sitting up in the basket looked a good deal better but was still giving Coffin a cold stare. Which was hard, he thought, as he was the cat lover.

'Watch it, cat,' he said. 'You're only here on approval.'

'Oh no, she isn't.' Stella was quick. 'This is her home now.'

'And she's not pregnant?'

'He says not.' Stella was quick to pick things up; she now sensed that all was not well with Coffin. 'What is it? Is Black Jack dead?'

'Not as far as I know.'

'So what is it?'

'It's a bloody, violent business that I can't see the way

through. That's not how it usually is with me. I'm used to knowing the way. I don't mean I always know the answer, because I don't, but I always feel the way to go.'

'All the deaths are the work of one killer, aren't they, though?'

'Yes, I think so.' He sat slumped in his chair; the kitten from her basket stared at him.

Stella came over, stroked the cat, then touched Coffin's forehead. 'You are a bit hot.'

'I'm not ill,' he said irritably.

Stella looked at herself in the looking-glass over the fireplace and smoothed her hair. 'I'm off to the theatre. I have a production meeting. Shouldn't last more than an hour. We'll eat when I get back. I'll leave you to look after the cat.' At the door she added, 'There's cold chicken if you get hungry and can't wait.'

Coffin looked at the cat. 'I don't fancy cold chicken, do you?'

The cat's expression did not change.

'I don't suppose you ought to eat it anyway, you being so small. Special cat food, something like that.' He went down the staircase to the kitchen. As he passed, he stroked the kitten's head. 'Come on, say something. Say you would help me if you could.'

The telephone rang. The house phone, not his mobile. The number was supposed to be protected, secret, but Stella was quite reckless in the way she passed it out. Business, she said.

'Hello.'

There was silence.

'Who is that?'

Distantly, he heard a laugh, and, 'Gotcha, Coffin.'

Then a voice said, 'I hate you, Coffin.'

Coffin did not answer. And you aren't the only one. I am not universally loved. Au contraire.

The voice started again: it was very soft, distant. But I can bear it, Coffin thought, I have been here before.

'I may include your wife in this.' A noise like a laugh. 'Thinking about it.'

Coffin put the telephone down while the voice was still talking, softer now, more like a whisper.

Walker? Was that the word? Or just walking? Or did he say he hated the Walkers? And softly, a word that sounded like babies. Hate for the babies? He debated whether to report the call. It would probably be pointless but, on the other hand, if he didn't report it and anything happened, he would be at fault. Moreover, Stella had been mentioned. Yes, he must report it.

Sergeant Marsh on the Aware desk – a name given by Coffin himself to a unit dealing with threats to anyone – was the one to call. He duly did so.

'Right, sir, see what we can do,' replied Marsh, courteous and helpful as always. You have to sound confident and cheerful, he had said once, it's part of the job, even though you know there's not much chance of your getting anything positive done. You can perhaps trace a phone call or an anonymous letter or someone leaving filthy rubbish on your doorstep or daubing your wall, but clearing up the emotion that lies behind it – well, that's different.

'Miss Pinero was mentioned, so I have to take it seriously.'

'I always do, sir.'

And so he did. But serious, with what you might call forward action, was not always possible, however much he saw the need for action.

'Let me know what you get . . . if anything,' said Coffin.

Marsh agreed that he would certainly do so, sir.

When Stella came back, she was surprised to find Coffin pacing the room. The cat was asleep in her basket.

'I thought you'd be either asleep or drinking.'

'Oh thanks.'

'No offence meant,' Stella said, with apology in her voice.

'I'd be glad to think of your being either . . . I'll have a drink myself. You can get me one.'

She watched while he poured some wine, red and glossy. 'You must think I need building up. That's what claret does, doesn't it?'

He poured out another glass for himself, looked at the cat, wondered if cats drank claret, remembered that none he had previously known had done, and replied, 'So they say.'

'And you think that I need it?'

'I reckon I do,' he said unhappily. 'Stella, darling, I just don't see my way through this.'

Stella stared. 'You never call me darling, not when you are sane.'

'I'm mad, then.'

'What's it about, my love?'

'And you don't call me that unless you are flaming mad with me.'

Their eyes met and they both started to laugh. Coffin reached out and hugged his wife.

'The fact is that I had one of those threatening telephone calls while you were out.'

'Here?' She was surprised, the number of their St Luke's home was private. Supposed to be; she always had guilty feelings about how casual she was with it.

'Yes, that's interesting. He got it somehow.'

'It was a man?'

Thoughtfully, Coffin said, 'I think it was. Not a very deep voice.'

'In my craft we know what you can do with voices,' pointed out Stella. 'I wish I'd heard. I might have been able to tell.'

'You can listen to the recording.' There always was a recording. He hesitated, 'I ought to tell you, there is a threat against you too.'

As always she could surprise him. 'Well, I'd guessed that. You wouldn't be floundering around in this way if it was only you.'

'It's what's known as the male protective syndrome,' he said apologetically.

'It has happened to me before,' Stella reminded him. 'Remember the thug who tried to rape me, and Gus and I bit him? And the Barlow twins? Sue Ann would have killed me if she could. She did have a go.'

The Beautiful Barlow Twins, so called by the media, had been torn apart by the jealousy Sue Ann had felt for Bobby Barlow's interest in Stella. Bobby and Sue Ann Barlow were acrobats and specialist dancers performing in Stella's Experimental Theatre during the Christmas season three years ago. Their father was Bert Barlow, the poet, so they were known as the intellectual acrobats, and indeed part of their performance was taken from Indian and Chinese sources. Stylistically, anyway.

Twins claim a special relationship, closer than ordinary siblings, which Sue Ann demonstrated by resenting any other woman who came close to Bobby. Quite a few did, as he was a lad with a wide range of tastes in styles, age and sex, which perhaps added a touch of sourness to Sue Ann's jealousy when his feeling for Stella became loud, strong and persistent.

'Still, she wasn't the worst one, although she did threaten to strangle me. Made it sound very real, that threat. Still, I knew it would end at the close of the season when Bobby forgot me.'

'I think she was worried that you wouldn't forget him,' said Coffin wryly. He had not enjoyed the episode of the Heavenly Twins (their stage name).

'No fear there. No, the worst was the nameless voice that would ring with hate threats. I did dislike him. It was a him, I think.'

'Yes, that wasn't nice,' said Coffin with a frown. 'Just stopped, didn't it? Marsh thought it was probably the chap whose body was floating in the river about that time. He had a bad mental history . . . You never let me know how frightened you were.'

Stella just shrugged.

'Nor did you tell me that Sue Ann had a go.'

'That was theatre business,' said Stella; she had very strong proprietary feelings where her theatre was concerned. 'Not a very serious attempt. Bobby stopped her. That was what she wanted really, proved how much she mattered to him.'

'I would have killed her if she had touched you.'

'That would have helped ticket sales, wouldn't it?' said Stella. 'It was at Christmas too. Finances were on a knife-edge that season.'

Coffin gave her a long, searching look, and apparently was satisfied with what he saw there. 'Devil,' he said fondly.

All the same, he told himself as Stella went to be womanly in the kitchen to work out what they would eat, all the same, I will watch over her.

And the Security Outfit of the Second City Force would watch over them both. But cynically, sometimes he wondered how much that meant. He had the impression that the same selective behaviour was going on in the Lumsden case.

They were going slow, seeing the best side of things at present. Maybe they didn't like Lumsden all that much as a person, but he was one of them, and that counted.

Like if I killed Stella, Coffin told himself; they'd knock themselves to bits proving it was an accident or that she did it herself in a clumsy moment.

He walked into the kitchen, where Stella was standing in front of the freezer looking thoughtful. Housekeeping was not her strongest point.

'We can eat out,' said Coffin.

Stella shook her head. 'No, I can put something together.'

Coffin's spirit sagged. He took his eating seriously. Something put together sounded depressing. Silently and without complaint, he left her to it.

The gods seemed to be indicating how he should fill in the time, so he dialled Inspector Fisher's Incident Room way over the other side of Spinnergate. Someone would be there, even if the Inspector himself was not. Fisher handled in person all important missing people, of which the Second City had more than the usual supply.

Fisher was there, however, and prepared to be grumpy at being disturbed when he was on the point of going home, except that the moment he recognized the Chief Commander's voice he changed, not to sweetness, that not being in his nature, but to great courtesy.

'Evening, sir. You've been getting our reports, I hope?'

'Oh yes.' And nothing much in them.

'The main thing is that Lumsden wants to come to work . . . says that the postcard proves his wife is alive and off because she wants to be. He claims she must have a lover.'

There was a question in Fisher's voice. He wants me to decide this question, Coffin thought. For a moment he was silent, then the warning bird came to sit on his shoulder.

'Leave it for another week or so. Say two weeks.'

Fisher came back promptly. 'Yes, sir, just what I thought myself.'

He's glad I've taken him off that particular hook, Coffin thought. It's what he wanted. The signal here was clear: Fisher was not convinced of Lumsden's innocence. In fact, probably just the opposite: he thinks Lumsden is guilty. Guilty, at the very least, of frightening away his wife, and, at the worst, of killing her and hiding the body.

Well hidden too, Coffin thought sourly.

Stella reappeared with the news that the meal was ready. A succulent smell followed her up the stairs. Coffin was surprised: salads and coffee, Stella was good at, but not food that smelt so tasty.

He gave her a suspicious look. On the kitchen table, a hot pie was surrounded by an array of vegetables, which had the look, so strange to English eyes, of being all different colours and shapes and only half cooked.

Stella saw him looking. 'Good for you to chew your vegetables.'

'Yes,' agreed Coffin, helping himself. 'As long as they don't bite back. I broke a tooth on that parsnip last week.'

'Does it taste good, that's what counts?'

'Who cooked it?'

'Max, or his kitchens in the Experimental Theatre.'

Experimental food too, was what Coffin thought, as he chewed on a thick slice of baked tuna.

'What are you giving your godson as a christening present? It's only days away, you know.' The question was malice to a degree, since Stella knew that Coffin had chosen no present nor even thought of one.

But Coffin was a quick thinker. 'Oh, money. A cheque to his mother to be banked until he is old enough to want it.'

'That won't be long,' said Stella. 'They start needing spending money as soon as they can toddle.'

Coffin got his revenge. 'I'll add a little toy, one of those soft ones; you can shop for that, if you will, please.'

'I don't like you when you are in one of these hard, clever-clever moods, and I can hear one coming along,' said Stella thoughtfully. 'I was only trying to jolly you along, cheer you up.'

'I wasn't being clever, just worried. This threat business. How did anyone get our number? Did you give it to anyone?'

'Not since the last time it was changed,' said Stella. This was true, but it was also true that she scribbled the number on numerous pads and odd bits of paper for her own convenience. I can't remember everything, she told herself.

'Things do get about,' she said vaguely.

'Oh, Stella.' It was a reproach, but the telephone number could soon be dealt with. 'I can get you a walker with dog. Just to see you through the next few days, while we see how things go.'

'No, thank you,' she said with decision. 'I suppose we ought to have another dog, if Gus should die, but I can't bear to think of replacing darling Gus when he isn't dead.' Ill, but not dead.

'I'd run behind you if I could,' said Coffin with mournful savagery.

Stella was still defending herself. 'If someone is hating us, it's better to know. That's reasonable, isn't it?'

'You don't understand how the process works,' said Coffin gloomily. 'A successful call like that this morning may be just his need to turn fantasy . . . because a lot of such calls are fantasy . . . into reality. Make it something hard that the caller can visualize.'

Stella removed the plates, noticing that her husband had, after all, made a good meal, and placed cheese and fruit on the table.

'When we go to the christening, you'll see Archie Young again.'

'Archie and Gus, both gone,' said Coffin sadly.

'Archie is not dead, and neither is Gus,' reminded Stella with some sharpness, 'and this is a christening, my love, not a funeral.' She took some cheese. 'You get champagne at a christening. Drink a lot of it, it'll take your mind off your troubles. And don't worry about drinking and driving. I shall hire a car: Sid Gubbins.'

Sid did all her driving in the district; in London she used the tube and cabs.

Sid Gubbins accepted the date, wrote it in his work diary, and told his wife.

'You can come too, make a day out of it. Miss Pinero will say yes, she never minds that sort of thing, you've been before. Be nice to see the Chief Super again – Chief Commander now.'

Sid was a retired policeman who had known Archie Young when he was a young sergeant. Mrs Gubbins, May Ann Gubbins, was a nurse, who went into the hospital when they needing extra nursing help. She was just coming to the end of her stint; a day out would be welcome.

I'll get my hair done, she told herself.

* * *

Next day CI Phoebe Astley made her report to the Chief Commander. Nothing much to say, nothing fresh; in fact she had the feeling the team was making very little progress on the three sets of deaths, Mrs Jackson and her daughters, Dr Murray, and Black Jack, that were connected by the gun. She covered this up, of course; no need to tell the Chief Commander what he would soon think for himself. In due course there would be inquests that would be adjourned to allow the police teams to work on.

Phoebe had worked closely with Archie Young and taken an interest in his son and even more in the son's wife, a talented young officer. She had been invited to the christening, but had pleaded another engagement. The truth was that she was at the age when she found christenings painful: she could still have had a child, but who was to be the father? So she had chosen a small teddy bear as a present instead.

Sergeant Tony Davley had worked with Sally Young; they had been rivals. She hadn't been asked to the christening, but she too had sent a present. A bit of silver, a christening mug of the early nineteenth century.

Tony Davley was gloomy about the chances of solving the several murders. It'll be one of those cases that runs and runs, she thought. The CI has got this pegged as a case of serial murders – she likes to put things in neat packets – but I don't see this case that way. Something else. I can sense it.

Tony sat in the canteen drinking coffee while she told the motherly figure of WPC Winifred Darby of her disquiet. She wrinkled her nose, 'I smell blood.' She drank some coffee. 'We're getting nowhere, but the CI doesn't see it.'

'Astley's not got much imagination,' said Winifred Darby. She looked at her watch. Her small son would be out of school soon, but her mother would collect him, and then her husband, it was his turn, would later take Benjy home. They divided the care of their son between them.

'Minus, minus,' agreed Tony.

In this they were both unfair to their superior officer, since Phoebe was uneasy. She too smelt blood.

*   *   *

On the late afternoon of the following Monday, Winifred was walking her dog. They enjoyed this walk, he in the gutters and at the street corners, and Winifred observing the life on the streets. She did not always take the same route, but varied them to match her mood. Spinnergate High Street was stocking up for Christmas. Had done so since October, well ahead of time as usual. Still, she found herself admiring some of the windows, gay, full of colour, even beautiful. It reminded her of her youth; unlike many, she had enjoyed being a child. Another butcher had closed. People still ate meat, though they didn't buy it in butchers' shops any more but in supermarkets or in Marks and Spencer, where the butchers wore white hats. Very dignified, but not what you expected when you were looking for a pair of tights.

Winifred did a lot of her personal shopping in such big stores, but she did not wish to be exposed to the smell of meat or fish as she did so.

She looked around for the dog who, as so often, had taken himself off. 'Tim, Tim, where are you?'

There he was at the end of the road, sniffing around the wheels of a small bus that she recognized as the Happy Days Nursery school bus. She knew Happy Days since her son had been a pupil there.

'One of their late-afternoon outings,' she pronounced as she walked towards it. The infants, some no more than three years, were taken swimming, to concerts and even to the theatre, where Stella Pinero put on special shows for children in the Experimental Theatre. Tickets were free. Get 'em young, was Stella's maxim.

The driver was out of the bus and standing in the road, studying the windows. Shattered, as Winifred could see as she came closer. Badly cracked, anyway; it was specially strengthened glass.

'What is it, Mrs Pomeroy?' she knew the driver, Betty Pomeroy, who had been a nurse once, and also the other

101

teacher, Nancy, who was inside the coach calming the children. As she spoke, she reached down to grab Tim's collar, who gave her a resentful stare in return.

'Oh, it's you, Win. Some lout threw a stone as we passed and broke that window.'

Win frowned, pulling hard at Tim's collar. 'Did you see him? I suppose it was a boy?'

'No, I did not see him,' said Betty with emphasis. 'I had my mind on keeping the bus straight on the road and not crashing it.'

'You'll have to report it,' said Win, her official face on.

'I will, you can count on that, but right now I have the kids to get back to the school, where the parents are waiting. None of the infants was hurt, thank goodness, but what an ending to an afternoon with the fairies.'

Win blinked.

'Not the sort you're thinking,' said Betty, climbing back into the driving seat. 'Although they may have been, this lot were dressed in blue and with wings. It was a nice little play though, with music; they all sang, audience and all. Not me, though.'

'Look for that pebble,' called Win. 'Would you like me to look? No?' She could see Betty shaking her head. 'Be sure you do it.'

'Oh, we will,' shouted Betty over her shoulder. 'You can bet. And if it's got the chap's name and address on it, then I will go round and kill him.'

'You do that,' said Winifred under her breath. She released her grip on Tim's collar, and together they continued on their walk. Sid Gubbins, doing an early-evening job, passed Winifred and Tim. He knew them both. He had worked on several cases with Winifred before his retirement; she was a decent sort, with a good brain and steady nerves. Kind heart too. She had been good to him when his son was missing in the Gulf War.

He waved his hand and Winifred waved back, as she plodded on with Tim, dragging the dog, who wanted to roam free to investigate, analyse and add to all the interesting smells. But Winifred wanted to get home to her husband, Harry, a CID sergeant working at Headquarters. He was an easy-going professional. He listened to her recount what had happened to the nursery school bus.

'You tell a good story,' Harry said. 'You're worried, aren't you?'

'Yes, and I'm not sure why. Result of talking with Tony Davley, I dare say. She's practically in tears over the lack of progress in the murders of the Jacksons and Dr Murray . . . she sees them as one.'

'Well, they are, aren't they?' said her husband, in a matter-of-fact way. He collected facts, old and new, since he was with one helper in charge of the registry of records. 'But I would like to know what the victims have in common, apart from the way they were killed.'

'Yes, I think that was worrying Tony, but she says she can't make out what Phoebe Astley thinks about it.'

'Astley keeps her thoughts to herself,' observed Sergeant Darby. 'But yes, I reckon there is a connection; there always is, you know, when you look hard enough, something that pulls the killer towards the victims. The way they smell perhaps . . .'

'In that case, Tim will be the one to consult, he's great on smells . . .' He had certainly been smelling the school bus.

Tim looked up as she spoke and gave a small growl. Surely suppertime was coming up?

'You know the niece or cousin or whatever, the girl they call Nat, don't you? Why don't you ring her up and have a talk with her?'

'I didn't know her well . . . we went to ante-natal classes together. I don't know what happened to the baby; I think it died.'

'Sometimes I wish ours had.' He raised a loving eyebrow at the noise of the six-year-old in the next room.

Win shook her head. She had had a miscarriage or two her-self and knew the pain they had both felt. Jokes were out.

He reached out, squeezed her hand, even as a tremendous crash came from the next room. He got up. 'My turn to see what he's broken this time.'

It had been his idea that they should divide looking after the child between them. He hadn't wanted Win to give up her career, even if it meant they saw less of each other because he was on duty while she was babysitting. And vice versa. But it had worked, and was working still. 'You belonged to that club, didn't you?'

'Yes,' Win smiled. 'The Walkers Club . . . Remember, we were going to walk the kids in their prams . . . for company; we did it for a bit before the kids came, although I was the size of the elephant's grandmother, as you may recall. Afterwards I was so sore I could hardly walk, let alone push a pram. The club sort of folded.' She smiled reminiscently. 'My stitches hurt like hell.'

'No need to tell me. I couldn't make love to you for weeks. More efficient than the pill.' The noise from the next room had quietened, and they could him singing. So, no one was dead. You always had to make sure. 'Small group, wasn't it?'

'Yes, but not just me and Nat; there were Sheila Fish and Letty Brown . . . Lia Boston . . . can't remember any more. For a little while I used to see those two shopping, and we'd have a laugh about the Walkers Club. Goes back to before we all discovered that there was more to looking after a baby than pushing a pram. Sheila had twins, so she found out first. All gone now. I'm too busy, life moves on and connections break.'

But connections are not so easily broken as Win supposed. Even though she herself never saw the Walkers, some of them kept up with each other.

Sheila Fish and Letty Brown (now remarried and Letty Onslow, but still Brown to her friends) met almost every week in the local supermarket that they patronized, where they would be joined in its coffee-shop by Lia Boston. Lia had been very unmemorable in those days, skinny and shy, but she had changed since then, dyed her hair, shortened her skirts, and developed expensive tastes. Her husband had become one of the most well-known petty criminals in the Second City.

The store where they met was broad-minded and commercially hard-headed enough to have a kind of car park for prams and a nursery where babies could be left for an hour – longer than that and you were in big trouble and might never get in again. Lia had tried once, so she knew.

Over coffee, the trio joked and gossiped.

'More Pushers than Walkers now,' commented Letty.

'You can do a deal of walking behind a pram,' pointed out Sheila.

'Never mind,' said Lia. 'Soon outgrowing prams. My eldest goes to that nice little nursery school every day now.' She looked at her watch. 'Going out on an outing by bus to the theatre. Billy Boy loves it.'

'Crime must pay', was in the look exchanged between the other two as they observed her watch and clocked up the fees at that 'nice little nursery school'.

They started with the missing Mrs Lumsden, where the verdict was that any woman had a right to walk out on her husband if she chose, with Lia contributing the comment: especially if he was a policeman, she did wonder. They hushed her at this point, moving on to the murders in Spinnergate, where they had a personal interest.

'Mrs Jackson delivered my baby,' said Letty. 'Kind, kind lady.'

'I went to her ante-natal class,' said Sheila. 'I found the exercise real tough, and she helped me. I can't bear to think of her being shot. Who would do it? And why?'

'Horrible,' said Lia, with a shudder. 'My Tom thinks there's more behind it than we know. A cover-up. Look at the police, he says.'

'Your Tom always blames the police,' pointed out Letty. 'But they can't cover up all the time.'

'Always Mrs Lumsden,' muttered Lia, determined and

dogged. 'Makes me nervous . . . my Tom says he has a good idea who did Mrs Jackson in, but I'm not to say anything in case it gets me into trouble too.' Trouble being death. She didn't quite believe him, Tom talked that way. 'I've kept up with the hospital because I go to the clinic and you don't. Joe Bottom is very nice, and so is his wife. I've got to be a friend of his daughter too.' So I am well informed. 'Don't need telling, I've got an independent mind, always have had, I remember my mum saying, "You always know your own mind, Lia, and good luck to you."'

'Your Tom told you though?' Letty persisted.

'Tells me everything. He had to go away and he wanted me to be on my guard.'

'How would he know?'

'Knows people, like Jack Jackson . . .'

'Who doesn't? So, where's your husband off to?' asked Letty, who always wanted to know the detail.

'America,' said Lia proudly.

Her mobile phone rang in her bag; she fished it out and listened, exclaiming as she did so.

'Must dash,' she said to her friends. 'Some lout has thrown a stone at the school bus and my Billy Boy needs his mum.'

'Don't worry, Lia,' they called after her. 'No one will ever kill you and your kids.'

Laughing, they returned to their coffee.

Coffin and Stella set off early for the christening of Archie Young's grandson the following Thursday.

Sid was driving, his wife in the front next to him, while Coffin sat in the back beside Stella reading various documents and letters, part of the workload that always seemed to go everywhere with him.

'How are things going?' Stella asked.

'Not a lot of progress yet. Goes like that.' This was the voice of experience. 'Days, weeks sometimes, of nothing much, then it comes with a rush.' He added: 'Any likely names have been checked.' Joe Bottom had been prime suspect for one of the murders, just because he had found Dr Murray's body – 'Always check on the finder of a corpse, ten to one the finder is the killer' was written on all crime officers' hearts. He had been looked over and found clean. No blood on him, and with other people at the time when Dr Murray had been killed. No motive, either, although with this killer, did that count? Jack Jackson would have been a prime suspect of the first murders of Mrs Jackson and her daughters if he had not been attacked himself. A puzzle, that attempt, Coffin frowned, then pushed the worry aside. For the time being.

'Off the leash for a day,' he said happily, while reflecting that it would not be difficult to know where they were going: he always had to leave the address behind him. Same for Stella, probably. She too always had a crisis on the boil. He seemed to remember notes with her whereabouts floating around or pinned on boards. So they were never really lost.

Stella reached out and put her left hand on his wrist. 'Easy ride?'

He turned to her with a smile. 'Easy ride. Happy day.'

She gave his wrist an affectionate pat, then went back to her reading.

Presents and her pretty hat were on the seat beside her.

8

Thursday.

'Are we lost?' asked Coffin. They had been driving for about an hour. For most of that time he had been absorbed in the work he had with him, leaving the driving to Sid Gubbins and route-finding to Stella.

'No.'

'We've been down this bit of road at least once before.'

'I didn't think you noticed.'

'Not the first time, but I remember it now.'

'Perhaps we were a bit lost, but I've found the way again . . .' She consulted the map. 'We follow this road, and take the left turn, it should be called Church Road . . . and it is. There is the church . . . you can see the spire.'

'I don't believe you were ever lost at all,' accused Coffin. Sid and Mrs Gubbins in her smart new hat were both tactfully quiet.

Stella let them drive on in silence for a minute, before saying, 'You're right, of course. I suppose that's what makes you a good detective: you can see into people, through them.'

Then he saw the tears in her eyes. Not theatrical tears, which she could contrive so beautifully, but real, painful tears that were reddening her eyes. They were not running down her cheeks; she was controlling the tears in her eyes. Only an actress could do that, thought Coffin.

'You don't need to say anything. I understand. I feel the same. But I can't cry. I wish I could.'

'It's hard for men.'

'Oh, they can cry all right, you know that, but I was born dry.'

'It's the baby, and Sally being so brave about it.'

Coffin nodded wordlessly. He was thinking of Charlie and his father, Archie Young. Charlie had reminded Coffin of himself when young.

The church in Wibberly was not particularly old, mid-Victorian, and built of red brick, but it was surrounded by well-kept grass and neatly weeded paths. In the churchyard lay several rows of graves: Charlie Young had not been buried here, for which Coffin was grateful.

Sid Gubbins parked the car at the end of a row, then got out to open the door for Stella, who was adjusting her hat. Mrs Gubbins got out too; her hat seemed indestructable and immovable.

Coffin fiddled with his tie. 'I didn't know what to dress for: a funeral or a wedding.'

'Something in between,' said Stella, checking her makeup. 'Serious but not sombre, offering a welcome to the new life.'

'Leave the presents in the car?'

'Yes. After all, it's not Christmas.'

They walked towards the porch door, where a small group were standing: grandparents, four of those, and the one parent, Sally, holding the child. The Gubbinses took themselves into the church, where they chose a suitable pew. They enjoyed being unobtrusive and tactful. Stella knew and enjoyed this too; she said it made her feel like the Queen with an equerry and a lady-in-waiting.

Archie Young came forward, hand outstretched. He had not changed, no greyer, no more lined. Grief had passed through him and out again, like a purge. He gripped Coffin's hand and kissed Stella on the cheek. 'Good to see you both. Thanks for coming.'

'In good time, I hope.'

'Very good. The vicar's just getting ready for us.'

Sally was nearby, the baby in her arms, awake with alert, bright blue eyes and red cheeks.

Healthy, Stella thought, thank goodness. She put out a finger to stroke the cheek. 'Hello.'

The child stared back from his nest of white wool, pressed against his mother's pink tweed suit. Sally was hatless, but her own mother, coming to greet Stella, was wearing a red hat to match her red suit. She was a pretty woman, smaller and slighter than her daughter, a doctor, now retired.

Maisie Young, who had been talking to the Chief Commander, kissed Stella's cheek. 'Lovely to see you.'

'You too. You are missed in Spinnergate.'

'I miss it too. It was home for such a long time, and Archie enjoyed working with the Chief Commander.'

'Archie deserved a top job.'

'He does love it,' admitted Maisie.

Their eyes met. Stella put her arm around Maisie, who let the happy mask drop for a second. 'Yes, well, Charlie's death hit us both hard . . . but we want to make today happy, for Sally's sake. She's been splendid. She's going back to work, you know.'

Stella nodded. 'I know.'

'She's taking her full leave, of course.' Maisie smiled as she looked at her daughter-in-law and her grandson. Sally was talking to the Chief Commander. 'She feels she has to be the success for both of them now.'

'I'm sure she'll do it . . . John thinks well of her.' And he likes a pretty face; mustn't be cynical. But Sally was clever, Stella knew something about her life before the police: a first-class degree from University College, London, and then a couple of years studying law. Yes, she'd climb the ladder all right, even with a baby on her back.

The child stared at Stella. 'All right, I'm thinking about you, chum.' He almost said it aloud; he had quite a commanding gaze that baby, for one so young. You look all right, he was saying, but I don't know you well enough to be sure. Babies have to be careful.

The pair were interrupted in their silent conversation by the arrival of the rector. Just as well, decided Stella, as the infant's mouth drew down, clearly deciding she was undesirable company. Or possibly it was the rector who was getting the dour looks.

He introduced himself: Paul Rudkin. Then he went over to speak to Coffin, murmuring that he knew he was a bit late starting, but with four kids you were never on time for anything.

'He never would be,' said his wife, Marie, coming up behind. 'Children or not.' She shook her head. She held out her hand, introducing herself and explaining that Sally had asked her to be godmother to the child. 'Time-keeping is not Paul's greatest gift.' She gave him a loving smile. 'Four kids, all under seven. You'd think an obstetrician would know better.'

'That's your job?'

'Will be again, I hope, when family life permits.'

'I admire you for doing it.'

'I admire you, Miss Pinero, or should I call you Mrs Coffin?'

'Either will do.'

'He's one too, you know, a performer. Mostly stage, but a bit of TV. Then he decided to join the Church, become a rector.'

Stella looked at the rector's blond good looks. Yes, she could see him as a performer. He still was, in a way.

His wife echoed her thoughts. 'Of course, the Church had use for his abilities. He knows it. But he may go back to the profession when he's got too old to be a rector.'

'Can you be too old?'

'In the time of Trollope, no; these days, yes.' Her eyes were on her husband. 'I think we are being instructed to go in.'

She was still talking as they walked in, following Sally with the child in her arms. 'Sally wanted it as quiet and simple as possible, although the christening service is not really elaborate anyway.'

Stella found Coffin at her side, and smiled at him. 'Nervous?'

'Do I have to hold the baby?'

'I think so, dear.' Then she relented, 'There is a godmother; she will hold the child, I expect.' She turned around. 'Two godmothers in fact, I'm told, unusual for a boy, so you get off lightly.'

'I don't see another,' worried Coffin.

'Just arriving. That's her car.' She nodded towards a little red Metro.

Coffin looked relieved. The sun came from behind a cloud as they walked into the church, the light following them in so that pews and altar and font were touched with gold. The double doors behind them were wide open, so a soft breeze came through to ruffle his hair and disturb Stella's fashionably bouffant hat.

They began with a prayer, then the organ offered up a quiet but happy melody; no melancholy for this child. Then a small choir, almost entirely made up of girls from the local school, sang a short anthem. They moved towards the font and the christening proper began. Coffin was not required to hold the child, but had to make the proper responses. The second godmother was a pretty young woman whom Coffin recognized as Sergeant Chrissie Miller, a member of the Second City Force. She had hurried in late, apologizing without explaining, thus causing Coffin to wonder what crisis had happened in his absence that he knew nothing of, but Stella, mind-reading as usual, managed to whisper in his ear, 'Just her soft contact lenses, could not get them in her eyes.'

Chrissie smiled, murmured what sounded like, 'Afternoon, sir, nice to see you,' turned to Marie Rudkin. 'Hi, fellow godmother. Who gets to hold the baby, Sal?'

'You for a minute.'

The infant was deposited in her arms, looked her in the face, and at once began to bawl.

For the first time Coffin felt he knew what the word bawl

meant, and he was glad, with an intensity that surprised him, that he was not the one provoking what was clearly anger.

But more to his own surprise, he was swept with a surge of sympathy for the creature.

'You're a noisy little customer,' said Chrissie, rocking the child in her arms. He just cried the louder.

'He's scared, I think,' said Godfather Coffin.

'Of course he is,' said Chrissie. She smiled at the rector, who was advancing towards them. He gathered up the infant and got down to business at the font.

Coffin, Chrissie, Marie Rudkin and the rector stood in a half-circle round the font.

Soon be over, Coffin thought, and like most happy occasions you will be glad when it is.

In the Second City, Nancy Eden had at last got round to cleaning the school bus. It was not a job she looked forward to, brushing and polishing not being one of her favourite tasks, but she had had the broken glass in the window replaced, and if she didn't do this cleaning she didn't know who would. Theirs was a small school that she and Betty Pomeroy had founded and owned together. It was now profitable, but only if both partners did a full share of the tiresome tasks such as setting out the milk and biscuits at break time, tidying up afterwards and overseeing the midday hot meal that came in from outside.

Cleaning the van fell in a doubtful category that both partners argued about, but this time it was clearly Nancy's task. After all, Betty with her medical training did the matron side of things, bandaging wounds and mopping up sick.

She was on her knees brushing the floor, where fragments of glass still lurked, dangerous to anyone but particularly so to small children. Apart from a genuine concern for the safety of her pupils' skin and eyes, Nancy knew that some of the parents of those children were litigious. Readily and eagerly so. Her own outfit had not so far suffered, but she knew that St Freda's down the road had suffered heavily. But then St

Freda's was an Academy of Dance, teaching ballet, where damage to limbs might almost be expected.

The light shone on a shard of glass under the long seat by the door. She always used this seat herself so she could keep an eye on the whole busload. She told the children who naturally sometimes tried to get there before her that she had to sit there in case she felt sick. Not true, and she doubted if they believed it, but a lie or two was sometimes necessary. You had to be devious on occasion when dealing with this age group.

She brushed up into her dustpan the small splinter of glass. Nearly done now, the floor and seats looked clear.

But something came bouncing into her pan after the glass. Nancy picked it out with a frown. She held it in her palm, clutching it with care.

'Well, I never.'

She went to sit on the long seat by the door where she had left her mobile phone.

'I'm no expert but I think I know what I've got here.' She felt the weight of it. A surprising density, for so small an object. Relatively small, she told herself; what do you want, a cannon ball? Not a pebble, not a nut, but a bullet.

'I'll tell Win Darby. If she's not at home, then her husband will be.' Nancy knew about the domestic and working arrangements of the two.

She dialled the number on her phone. 'Win? Nancy here. I'm sitting in the school bus . . . we were bombed.'

'What? Is this one of your jokes?'

'No, well, bomb perhaps isn't the right word. But it wasn't a stone thrown at the bus: we were shot. I've found the bullet.'

Win was quiet for second. Then she said decisively, 'Bring it round.'

Winifred Darby knew both Betty and Nancy, as well as the young girl who helped in the nursery class. She had always thought Nancy, pretty and fond of good clothes, the more phlegmatic of the two; now she wondered.

She opened the door to Nancy. 'Come in, I've made some coffee.' She looked into Nancy's face; she was white and pinched-looking. On the way round Nancy had had time to think about what might have been. 'I think you need something stronger than that.'

She poured some coffee, added brandy, and took the same herself. 'Show me what you've got.' She looked and nodded. 'Yes, it's a bullet.'

'I told you so.'

'You said bomb at first,' Win reminded her, glad to hear that Nancy's voice was stronger now.

'What are we going to do?'

'I'll show the bullet to Harry. He'll take it in to HQ.' She did not say so, but she thought that the team dealing with the series of shootings in the Second City would want to see it. She would talk to Sergeant Tony Davley herself.

'You must catch the gunman.'

'Oh, he'll be caught,' said Winifred with more confidence than she felt inside.

Nancy took a long drink of coffee. 'Been a lot of murders, Win, all with guns. I only know what I've read in the papers. Do you think this shooting could be connected?'

'Could be,' said Win patiently. 'Mustn't jump to conclusions. You'll have to answer questions about what happened. What did you see?'

Nancy thought about it. 'I didn't see much . . . I was talking to one of the children who had been crying . . .'

'They might have seen something.'

'Oh, I don't want them questioned,' said Nancy promptly. The school's finances were on a knife edge, so any rush of parents to take children away would have been a disaster.

'Don't worry,' said Win. 'Any questioning would be done very tactfully, parents present and everything.'

Nancy groaned inside. Parents were the last thing she wanted around, asking questions, fussing, some of the mothers crying, provoking similar tears in their offspring.

'We did report it at the time. You know we did.'

'Yes, I know, but then it was called just a silly, childish prank.'

'I never called it that,' said Nancy hotly. 'I always knew it was dangerous . . . and I was right.'

'Where is the bus now?'

'Where we garage it; at Steve Overshot's . . . he drives it for us sometimes.'

'I know his garage.' Win hoped he was not likely to hose it down because forensics would want to look at it. 'Did he repair the glass?'

'Yes.'

So his fingerprints would be all over the broken pane. But then no one had suggested that the gunman had come up to the bus close enough to touch.

'Do you think he will come back? Have another try?'

Win shook her head. 'It's nothing personal . . . the CID think he's just one of those chancers, no personal motive, just takes an opportunity when it offers.' She patted Nancy's hand. 'You leave it to me.'

'I sent her off happy,' Win said to Tony Davley. 'Well, happier.'

The two were meeting in the canteen by arrangement. Win had set up the meeting for the first hour of her return to duty. She had let Tony know that she had something to show her that might be very important.

She handed the bullet over, saying where it had come from, then she took a drink of coffee while she waited for the detective's reaction.

Tony did not leave her waiting long.

'I'll get the bullet checked to see if it could be a match to the ones that killed the Jackson family.' Already a mist of anonymity was descending over the dead Jacksons; just 'the family' now, nothing more personal. 'And Dr Murray.'

Win tried to probe. 'Any new developments?'

Sergeant Davley shrugged. 'We have a case meeting every morning, but nothing much so far. Forensics are moving at their usual pace but they seem to confirm that the same gun killed all the Jacksons and also Dr Murray, but why and how they were picked on . . .' She shrugged again. 'What is it? What's the connection? Is there one?'

Win waited. She sensed that Davley had something she wanted to say.

'She was killed in the museum of medical specimens. She was surrounded by a circle of skulls . . . infants' skulls. I don't know about you, but I don't like that.'

'Don't like the idea.' Win thought about it. 'Nasty picture. I didn't see it, of course, glad I didn't.' She studied Sergeant Davley's face. 'I suppose you did.'

For answer, Davley pushed a black and white photograph across the table. 'I'll deny that I ever showed you this.'

Win saw the body of Dr Murray lying spreadeagled on the floor of the museum. A pool of blood, which someone, Tony Davley she supposed, had outlined in red. Also outlined in red was the circle of tiny skulls. There was another bloody area nearer to the wall. This too had been circled in ink, black not red.

'Different blood,' said Davley. 'Believe it if you can.'

'Oh, I do . . . From the killer?'

Davley shrugged. 'Who knows? We don't. Not yet. When you've got a suspect, then you can try to match blood to him. Or her. But we haven't got a suspect.'

The process the CID team were doing at the moment was known as 'trawling', trawling the ground, as with a net, to see who and what they could pick up. Trawling sometimes dragged in likely characters, sometimes not.

'Where did you get this photograph?'

'Scrounged it from the SOCO photographer. He wasn't satisfied with it, as the background is blurred. He did another set, but from a different position. I thought they didn't show the position of the body so well.'

'So you helped yourself to the good one?'

'Sort of.'

Win wasn't quite sure if she believed that explanation, but

she wasn't going to argue. The background of the photograph was certainly blurred. Behind the body, to the side of one of the display cabinets, there was a pair of glass doors. A shadowy figure could just be seen peering through the window.

'Who's that?'

'I don't know. A hospital worker, I expect. The death caused quite a sensation. Whoever it is just wanted a look, I suppose.'

Win nodded. 'Hang on to that photograph.'

'Oh I will.'

'Who took it?'

'Eddie Chanlon, I think,' said Tony, still vaguely. 'I think.'

Sally Young patted her son's cheek dry. The infant stopped howling, and Coffin drew in a deep breath.

'That's done,' he said to Stella.

'Were you as bad as this with your own child?'

Coffin thought about it. 'I don't think we had him done. Just as well really, because I don't think any Christian god was interested in him; more likely one of the darker Egyptian deities would have suited him.'

'All these years together, and I'm still never sure when to take you seriously.'

'Always and never.'

'There you go again.' She was laughing, used to their familiar joking interchange. 'Noël Coward here we come. But better shut up, the rector may not find the joke funny.'

'Who said it's a joke?' said Coffin, but he said it silently, to himself.

His mobile phone rang in his pocket, and he dragged it out. 'Can't speak now.'

It was Tony Davley. He had to admit that she didn't fuss about nothing. 'You ought to hear this, sir. We've found a bullet that matches with the bullets in the killings.'

'Tell me later,' Coffin snapped.

They still stood in that same half-circle round the font; Sid and his wife moved up as well. All were staring towards the child with his mother, all had their backs to the door.

The organ was playing a happy anthem, above which the noise of the shot was almost inaudible. It came across like a passage of air.

Coffin spun round, turning towards the west door. 'Get down, all of you.'

Stella moved to protect her husband, putting her own body in front of him. 'Get down yourself.' Of course, it would be Coffin they were shooting at.

But it was Marie Rudkin who slid to the ground, her breast covered in blood.

9

Thursday onwards.

The Chief Commander and Stella Pinero were welcomed back in the Second City with a hushed, nervous enthusiasm, as if they had returned from a war.

On the way back, Coffin had telephoned the hospital to check on Marie Rudkin's condition; she was alive, but her condition was precarious. 'Still alive,' he said briefly to Stella, stuffing his mobile phone in his pocket.

A conference was called by CI Phoebe Astley, expeditious as always, in the Record Room, in which the leaders of the CID could meet in quiet surroundings with only files and video reels and tape-recordings, all neatly packed away and totally passive until disturbed by human action into giving up what they knew. In itself the Record Room was neutral.

Sergeant George Cummins was in charge today, Harry Darby being on leave. Both liked a quiet life, and usually got it. George had started out as a uniformed officer in Cutts Street Station, which was always in trouble, caused, so the police there complained, by the proximity of Nean Street, whose stocky, barrel-chested inhabitants were a tribe on their own. Very early on he had formed the ambition to move into the plain clothes side of police work and to establish a base in the HQ. He was a quiet, introspective man, who knew his limitations. He also knew that someone like him had a place in modern police work.

'I'm a documents man,' he told himself. 'I can do my

thinking best at the computer or with a folder of papers.' So he got himself a degree in social history at the Open University in his spare time. (Spare time? queried his long-suffering wife; tell me what that is.) He had made himself proficient in the world of the computers a decade ahead of his fellows, advised therein by his tutor at the Open University.

As Sergeant Cummins, BA, he was treasured as a unique specimen by his colleagues.

Into his quiet world poured a procession. First came Chief Inspector Phoebe Astley, and after her Inspector Paul Masters, Sergeant Tony Davley and other supporters. Other officers had stayed behind in the Incident Room.

'Sorry to break in,' said Phoebe. 'Can we park ourselves on you?' Not pausing for an answer, she sat down at a table in the window where a big computer was located, and nodded to her followers to do the same. 'Find the chairs.'

'You know why we are here: I wanted a quiet place to talk. Before we talk to the Chief Commander. He's had a bad time at the christening. Mrs Rudkin may survive, but we think the bullet was meant for him.' She turned to George. 'All right there, George?'

CI Astley was known for her trick of gathering up a congenial group of fellow officers to talk over a case with them. The Chief Commander was supposed to know nothing of this trick, but was alleged to have commented that he knew more that went on than she thought.

However, at this moment, he was still on the way home.

George nodded. 'The new shooting? Want me to clear off?'

Phoebe shook her head. 'No, stay.'

'Well, I won't interrupt.' But he said this to himself, turning away to pick up some of the folders that Phoebe had knocked off the table as she sat down. 'Clumsy cow,' he thought, again not aloud. In spite of this comment, he liked and admired Phoebe as a good officer. Tidy too; a set of documents sent out to Phoebe came back neat and in the correct order, not pulled to bits with coffee spilt on them. Also, she knew how to use the computer. She was literate in all the languages George admired, among which English was by no means the chief. His wife too admired CI Astley, saying that she would be the one to run to in any crisis, but then his wife had recently joined a women's group, which he suspected Phoebe was behind. His own feeling was that if there was any sort of crisis that involved being lost on a desert island it was Stella Pinero he would go to every time. He admired the Chief Commander, who had certainly created a highly efficient Force (after all, it employed George), but he had picked up comments that he took over in CID matters a touch too often . . . Or did he? He was a first-class detective. Anyway, he had got to the top, and George intended to do the same himself.

'I heard within the last few minutes that the Chief Commander is on his way back.'

A murmur of satisfaction or relief greeted her.

'He's okay.' Another murmur of pleasure. 'This shooting does not come within our patch – it's Southern Counties territory – but I'm sure we'll be co-operating.'

Another murmur. Yes, yes, yes.

'Stella is all right too. And we don't know yet if . . .' she paused, searching for the name, 'Marie Rudkin is going to pull through.'

The CI is really upset, Tony Davley thought. She's the one who never loses a name.

'We have had a run of murders by shooting: four. I think there may have been an attempt to kill a child or a teacher in a school bus – a bullet has been found that matches with those used in the killings. And now today we have this sixth shooting.'

'And it's all by the same man?' said Paul Masters, hardly making a question of it.

'I think so. It looks like it. Could be a copycat killing, except for the matching bullet. I have no doubt that this new attack is one of a series.'

'And does the gun used on Marie Rudkin match?' This was Tony.

'Don't know yet.'

So what are we doing here, Tony thought. In the main Incident Room a team of officers had been left behind. Sergeant Williams, WDC Peters, several others on computers taking messages and logging in others.

'I believe that the Chief Commander was meant to be the victim of this new shooting.'

Paul Masters spoke first. 'Is there any evidence of it?'

'Not yet, but I am sure we will get some. This run of shootings has been Second City only. Marie Rudkin was not Second City, so I think she was hit instead of the Chief Commander.'

'Oh, I don't know,' said Paul Masters. 'What does the Chief Commander think?'

'I haven't discussed it with him.'

Masters said thoughtfully, 'It could be Stella. She could have been the intended victim. In fact, it's more likely; this killer seems to go for women.'

'Don't forget Jack Jackson.' Jack was still alive, but only just. Death was round the corner with an open hand and beginning to grasp. Even as they spoke, Jack died.

'And then there's the school bus . . . children as victims?'

Phoebe said irritably. 'It's not a strict pattern, I'm not saying that.'

'The latest shooting was at a christening,' pointed out Tony. 'And a policeman's child. Sally's an officer, too, for that matter.'

'Not touched,' said Phoebe seriously.

'Either the killer's aim is bad or he's not into killing mothers with children.'

'You're not taking this seriously,' said Phoebe.

'Did you believe all that?' Tony said to Paul Masters as they filed out.

'I don't know.'

'One of Phoebe's gabfests. She has them sometimes.'

'What does that mean?'

'Oh you know: every so often she gets an idea in her head and wants to share. We made a captive audience.'

'So you don't believe the Chief Commander was meant to be shot?'

Tony shrugged. 'I don't know. Let's ask him.'

Coffin and Stella had come back together, both of them tense. Coffin spoke to Phoebe Astley on his mobile, asking her to set up a meeting for him. She had already created one meeting, but she kept quiet about that.

Stella watched as he phoned, but said nothing. She knew he was talking to Phoebe. I'm not jealous of that woman, of course I'm not. We inhabit different spheres. It's a working relationship for them both. But she knew they had been close, fairly close if the truth were told, in that period when she and Coffin had been far, far apart.

Sid drove them, his wife by his side. Neither of them spoke much.

'D'you think she'll pull through?' Sid murmured to his wife.

'Live, you mean?'

'Of course. You saw her, I never got close. Will she get through?'

She shook her head. 'I don't know.'

'I wish I knew what I could do.'

'Just drive, Sid,' said Coffin from the back.

'Sorry, sir. Didn't know you could hear.'

Coffin sank back into his seat. 'I wish I was driving now.'

Stella murmured that she was only too thankful he was not. He was a good driver when he was calm, but otherwise . . .

'And I'm not calm now?'

'Do you think you are?'

By his silence, Coffin admitted that he was far from calm. Eventually he said, 'It was the child. He could have been killed.'

'But he wasn't,' said Stella stoutly.

They finished what was left of the journey in silence. Stella was left at St Luke's Tower and Sid drove the Chief Commander on to his office. He wanted action.

He could see Paul Masters and Phoebe Astley in the outer office. He could read relief in their faces at the sight of him.

He was welcome. This wasn't always the case by any means.

'Glad to see you, sir,' said Paul. 'We heard about what happened. How is Mrs Rudkin?'

'She was taken into the Southern Counties Hospital . . . She was alive then.' Coffin nodded, still worried.

'I'll make a call, shall I, sir?' asked Phoebe. 'One of the surgeons there is a friend of mine.'

'Yes, do, Phoebe.'

She took herself into the outer office, dialling on her mobile.

'A rotten business,' said Masters. 'Thank goodness you weren't hurt. Did you manage to see the attacker?'

'No, we all had our backs to the door except Mrs Rudkin.'

'Perhaps that's why he aimed at her.'

'I don't know why he did. Even if it was a man . . .'

Masters looked surprised. 'Could it have been a woman?'

'I don't know,' said Coffin. He wanted to move on. 'What is the message that I got about the bullet found in the school bus?'

'It matches with the bullets used in the killings,' began Paul, but he was interrupted.

Phoebe returned to the room. 'Marie Rudkin has been taken to St Thomas's.'

'Sounds bad,' said Masters.

'No, I don't think so. Dr Rudkin worked in the hospital herself at one time, and before that the university hospital here. She'd feel at home. She's there for an operation. The nurse sounded quite cheerful.'

'That's her professional face.'

'Shut up.'

'Thank you for telephoning, Phoebe. I'll ring myself later. Or get Stella to . . . she might be best.'

'What's the position, sir? Are we in charge of the investigation into this new shooting?'

'No, the Southern Counties Police are in charge . . . we will help out as requested and come in if the connection with the shooting here is established.' He added quickly, 'Of course, we will be in contact. Chief Inspector Dent will be in touch, Phoebe.'

Phoebe said she knew Geoff Dent and they could work together. He was a very efficient officer, knew when to break the rules and when not to. She wanted to get her hands on this killer. Or killers, she added thoughtfully in the notebook she was making. She felt there might be two.

'Yes, I'll ring Stella to tell her about St Thomas's. She can telephone. She might even go there.'

But before he could telephone his wife, Stella had called him: 'John, Mrs Tully has come in with the story that a neighbour and her three children have been found shot dead.'

'Sounds like a domestic,' said Coffin.

'The father is in America.'

'Since when?'

Sheila Fish always passed on to Lia a magazine that both enjoyed. Lia read it, then gave it to a charity shop. The magazine was called *For Women Only*.

Letty Brown did not care for the magazine; she said she wanted to broaden her mind, not narrow it, and she was going to take up French. Sheila said that if she looked at the magazine and saw the subjects its articles covered, she would see it was very broad indeed. Letty said she had looked at the magazine, and she was surprised that Sheila read that sort of thing, and she was surprised the charity shop accepted it, but Letty said that the charity shop was keen to get it and that it always sold very well.

But now Sheila came to see Letty because she was worried.

'I took the mag round to Lia, but she wasn't there.'

'She's gone out shopping,' said Letty, not concerned at all and surprised at Sheila.

'But she said she'd be in when we spoke on the telephone this morning.'

'She's just popped out. She'll be back. Try again.'

Sheila said slowly, 'I think the door was on the latch.'

'And you didn't go in?'

Sheila shook her head. 'No, didn't like to.'

Letty put her hand on Sheila's shoulder. 'Go now.'

'Come with me.' Then she said, 'Please.'

Letty studied her friend's face. She saw this was something she had to do. 'Yes.'

Sheila said, 'We can't take the kids.'

Letty's mother lived two doors down the road. 'We can leave them with my mother. She won't mind if we aren't too long.'

The two women held hands as they approached the door of Lia's flat.

'It's open a crack,' said Letty. 'Was it like this when you came?'

Sheila nodded.

'You didn't try to go in?'

'No. I was frightened.'

They were both frightened, but holding hands they pushed open the door to walk into the hall. The smell hit them both as they walked in.

Their eyes met and Sheila dragged back, but Letty pulled her onward towards the sitting-room door, which was partly open.

Something was obstructing the door as Letty pushed against it.

Lia was lying, face down on the floor, her feet pushing at the door. She lay in a pool of drying, stale blood.

The children lay crouched together like little animals. But dead.

Dead, dead, dead.

Letty had said, 'We'll phone the police from here, then we'll go and wait outside.'

The telephone was working, to Letty's relief; it could have been cut. The police took in what she said and promised a car there at once.

Letty and Sheila waited outside, leaning against the wall. Mrs Tully, who knew them both, passed on the way back from the big shop on the corner.

'You all right? You look terrible.'

There seemed no reason not to tell her. Mrs Tully absorbed the news with surprise and horror.

'Children too?'

She stayed with them till the police patrol car arrived, then she left.

She wondered if Miss Pinero knew about it. She was on her way there now, to clean the silver.

'If she's there, then I shall have to tell her.' After all, she was married to a policeman. Well, *the* policeman really, and one for whom Mrs Tully had a healthy respect, since she cleaned his silver and her daughter had joined the Force last year, uniform of course, but hoping for a sideways move to CID in time. And her black Persian that had been lost had been brought home by the local copper. Nothing to do with the Chief Commander, of course, but it all added up.

She was surprised at the look of anguish that shot across Miss Pinero's face when she told her of the killings, and at the speed with which she telephoned the Chief Commander.

10

A terrible day continues.

'Phoebe Astley got there before me,' he confessed to Stella on the telephone. 'Clever woman.'

'Good job I'm not jealous of her then,' said Stella.

'No, you couldn't be that,' he answered seriously.

'Anyway, I've heard she prefers women.'

'Oh really?' said Coffin with interest. 'I hadn't heard.'

'I never know when to believe you,' said his observant wife.

Coffin laughed. He too had reserves of knowledge.

'I swear I could shoot you myself sometimes,' said Stella.

Coffin walked up and down his office while he made his announcement to his immediate staff, people he worked with all the time and trusted: Paul Masters, Phoebe Astley, DC Grahame Godley and their assistants, which included people such as DC Geoff Little. Inspector Lavender, still dealing with the Jackson murders but now increasingly involved in all the others, was also there. Tony Davley was not summoned, but she managed to slide in unnoticed. This was going to be an important meeting, and she meant to be in on it.

'I know you have had one meeting. A good idea, Phoebe, but don't think I am copying you. I call this the Crime Forum because it will be in existence until the murderer is caught.'

After some discussion Coffin decided that they should take over the Record Room once again, politely moving aside Sergeant George Cummins. Cummins did not mind, firstly because it was done by a courteous message delivered by Paul Masters, requesting the use of the room, and secondly because he was asked to keep the record.

'Tomorrow, early, Phoebe, all those who are here today and a few others.' He was already drawing up a list in his mind.

At least one officer was being plucked from every Incident Room, going back to the Jackson killings and now taking in the death of Lia and her children.

The shooting of Marie Rudkin was included, even though it was another county.

All the Incident Rooms were connected by telephone and fax, but what the Chief Commander called the Crime Forum would be the central meeting place.

Get in there quickly, the message went round the corridors, the Chief Commander is in a hurry. He must have been brewing this up for some time.

In fact, Coffin had thought about it even as he was driven back to the Second City by Sid. It had been a silent journey. No one wanted to talk.

'I don't know if this shooting is related to the others, but I am betting it is,' he had thought as the countryside slid by. 'It's got to be investigated as a whole. And I am going to be in charge.'

He had stared out of the window; they were on the outskirts of the Second City by then. Stella had been quiet. Then she said she could feel he was distressed, as she was herself. When she closed her eyes she could see Marie falling to the ground with the blood spurting out. But she felt something else as well with the Chief Commander. There was a hard set to his mouth, which he only showed when angry.

'Do you think that the bullet was aimed at you, then?'

'I don't know,' said Coffin, 'but by God I'm going to find out.'

Coffin began: 'We are going to have a Crime Forum. I call it that for want of a better name. I am calling in one or two important officers who have been working on these killings. They can no longer be considered in isolation. We must treat them as linked killings.'

There was a murmur of assent from his audience.

'All relevant information will be pooled here ... Yes, and some that might not seem relevant, because you can't always tell.'

Phoebe Astley muttered to herself that strict relevance had never been the rule; you had always had to keep your ears and eyes open to catch what might turn out to be important.

As the Chief Commander paused, the door swung open and a trolley of tea, coffee and mineral water was pushed in. Coffin was not surprised since he had ordered it.

He moved towards the trolley, and poured himself some coffee. 'Phoebe, can I pour you a cup? Tea or coffee? Help yourself everyone.'

He was following Stella's advice. 'Get on good terms with them at once ... Make it all easy, smooth ... You've been very tense lately, and it makes you tough on the people you work with.'

As he had talked about it to Stella on the way home, with Sid all ears, the idea of the Crime Forum had been born.

Now it was all around him. He had the people, and he had displays on big boards all around the room, one for each case, together with names and short bios plus photographs of all the people touched by each murder. And the tea wagon had arrived.

He looked at Phoebe Astley and grinned. 'Thanks, Phoebe, good organization.'

A telephone call had told CI Astley what he wanted. You never had to tell Phoebe anything twice. 'Glad to help, sir.'

'Keep a straight face, Phoebe,' said the Chief Commander. 'Sometimes I can read your thoughts.'

Stella had taught him how to do it. 'Don't look at the mouth. Watch the eyelids,' she'd said. 'If they come down too far, it's a giggle.'

'Wouldn't help much with an Oriental,' he said.

Stella had ignored this.

Coffin could see that CI Astley was half amused and half wondering what good he hoped to get from this meeting, yet she also knew he was not a man to look for personal advancement. Not in any obvious way, at least.

Over his coffee, he said, 'I must be in charge, Phoebe. I shall be making the announcement, not everyone may like the idea, and food and drink does help.'

He stood by the trolley for a time, drinking his coffee, and then began to move round the room.

Board A: The Jackson murders. Detective Sergeant Jim Ward. A plan of the flat was there, with marks where the bodies had rested. A photograph of Mrs Jackson's body. A bullet in a plastic bag. A trail of blood suggested she had been shot first and tried to reach her daughters, but she had died, choking on her own blood. A brutal business, said a note from Jim Ward.

Board B: Dr Murray. Detective Sergeant Annie Bertram. On this board was a similar plan of the body of Dr Murray. There was also a photograph. There was the blurred image of a face looking through a window in the further wall. The bullet in the plastic bag again. And the blood tests revealing blood from more than one person. The contents of her handbag were listed, the usual stuff that women carry, such as lipstick and powder. She carried a diary and a notebook. The contents of both had been transcribed, but appeared to be engagements and notes of work in progress. There was also the ring that had been found.

Board C: Jack Jackson, only recently a murder case. Sergeant Ward and WDC Morris. The usual photograph, an autopsy report . . . Jackson had been in good health. A list of the contents of his pockets. Money, keys, diary.

Board D: The school bus . . . not too much on this one. WDC Morris had spoken to all the children on the bus and made notes. More to come, no doubt. No one had been hurt on this occasion.

Board E: The christening. D C Parsons. A map of the district, a photograph (which Coffin had already seen) of the victim. The telephone number of the Southern Counties CID. Not much, so far, but Parsons was doing his best.

Board F: Lia and her children. D S Ireland. Again, photographs and sketches. The bullets in the bag.

In addition to all this, a bundle of witness statements, such as there were, had been pinned to the board.

'Dross,' Coffin said to himself as he read them, noticing with some amusement how carefully a way was cleared for him as he moved from board to board. 'No good. No one saw anything or anybody.'

He poured himself some more coffee while talking to one of the young detectives. He knew that although he was popular in the Second City Force, there were those who thought he was too active in the CID.

'It's an addiction,' he had heard someone say. 'He should stick to being a figurehead and leave the hard stuff to us.'

Jim Ward, that had been. And there was Jim, standing next to him while drinking coffee.

'Hello, Jim.'

'Hello, sir. Can I get you some more coffee?'

'No, I'm all right. How's your wife?'

Jim's wife was a young, efficient, industrious house surgeon at the local hospital.

'Working hard,'

'It's addictive,' said Coffin soberly. 'I know about that. I guess you do, Jim.'

Jim grinned. He knew he'd been sussed. 'She says she wouldn't mind if she never saw another Caesarean.'

'She shouldn't have settled for obstetrics.'

'She's good, sir.'

Coffin liked him for admiring his wife. 'I will have some more coffee, Jim. Black.' Looking round the room as he waited for his coffee, he realized that he had got together some of the brightest and most ambitious of young officers. His meeting had achieved that, at least. As he thanked Jim for the coffee, he wondered how ambitious Jim was, or if his ambitions were subsumed into his wife's. Perhaps you only needed one ambitious party. He thought about himself and Stella, where certainly his early ambitions and Stella's own had kept them apart. But somehow they had now achieved a working partnership.

Witness today's gathering. Would he have put it together if Stella had not injected him with a little of her theatricality? Because this was a staged occasion, and would go on being so.

He soon realized that he was not the only one doing a little staging. Each of the officers had attached his or her name to the board of evidence that had been put together and had accompanied their senior officer to the meeting.

Coffin reflected that he had not invited them, but that they had been very sensible in deciding to come. Clearly there had been communication between them and a common decision had been made.

Passing the board by which Jim Ward now stood, head erect, ready for questioning, Coffin said, 'What made you all decide to turn up?'

'Seemed right, sir.'

Coffin waited for more.

'Each of us wanted to see what the other teams were getting.'

'But you have ACE.' Access and Exchange was the system set up by Coffin himself. 'Information should be exchanged that way.'

Jim Ward met the Chief Commander's questioning face without expression. He said nothing.

'I see, silly of me, you don't exchange . . . or only what suits you.'

Coffin realized that he had been living in a rarefied atmosphere, on Mount Olympus, forgetting what life was like lower down. Well, I am getting to know the groundlings.

'Has it been worth it?'

'Yes and no, sir.'

Having inspected all the boards to see what the other investigating teams were up to, they decided that nothing very exciting had been handed over.

Which was what they had expected. Do you tell the other chap the results of your best work? No, not unless obliged.

Coffin knew this as well as anyone.

'Sit down everyone. Today is just a beginning. I shall want the records kept up to date . . . perhaps more fully than some are today.' Here he kept a straight face. 'Because I suggest they are studied daily. Each and every case. Because it is all one case.

'I am taking control of the investigation into the killings,' he said. 'They are linked.'

Only one voice was raised in question. 'Can we have copies of the file of evidence in each case, and photographs?' It was D S Annie Bertram, who was dealing with the death of Dr Murray. 'If I have to regard the deaths as connected, then I want to have all that's to hand . . . It's not very much,' she allowed herself to say.

'More may be added,' Coffin said.

'And I'd like to see the photographs, if copies can be given.'

'Yes,' said Coffin. He looked at Phoebe Astley.

She had been prepared for this. 'It's in hand.'

'Good.'

'And I think a suitably censored report of this meeting ought to be given to the press,' said Phoebe.

'Yes. I'd like the killer to know we are all after him. Or her.'

There was a moment's silence. 'You can't believe this killer is a woman?' said Phoebe.

Coffin said, 'Somewhere in the files you are putting together is the name and face of the murderer. I believe that.'

Then he said, 'And include your own photographs.'

There was a stunned silence in the room.

Coffin let the moment run without interrupting it. He

enjoyed the second or so it lasted. They're working out whether it's a joke or whether I mean it, and deciding I do.

Jim Ward allowed himself a joke. 'I don't take a very good photograph, sir.'

'A passport photograph will do,' said Coffin, unsmiling.

Jim Ward abandoned the joke and decided to be brave. He could live on his wife's earnings. 'And will you submit a photograph, sir?'

Coffin looked at CI Astley.

'One is already preparing,' she said with a straight face.

Coffin had no idea if this was true or not, but it fitted in with what he was about to say.

'You see now what I want: when we come into the Record Room daily to see what is on the boards, I want us to feel we are walking into a large room with the victims and the murderer all around us. We are in the middle, watching the story grow.'

'Sounds like new science,' said Annie Bertram, who had a son at school.

'I believe we should get an answer,' said Coffin. 'And whoever gets there first, then I hope you will tell me. DI Masters and DCI Astley are the channels to use.'

Sergeant George Cummins was taking notes and using his tape-recorder; he would like to have taken a photograph of the proceeding, moving if possible. He decided he must ask the Chief Commander if he could do this on another occasion. It wasn't the sort of thing you did without asking him. He presumed he would always be the record keeper.

Questions were coming in now. DC Geoff Little said that he had been part of the team working on Dr Murray's murder and he was worried about the heads found arranged round her. Couldn't see a reason.

'Not a reason,' said Annie Bertram. 'This killer is not reasonable.'

'Mad, you think?' asked Coffin.

'Yes, probably, sir, and that ought to help us to find him.'

Geoff Little said that he had been told about the discovery of the skulls of the Neanderthal babies. 'Was there a connection?'

'Possibly,' said Coffin. 'There was also a more modern head. Forensics have been working on that. So far, nothing to use in the current cases; may have no connection.'

There was a murmur from the rest. This was something they all wanted to know. There was a bubble of questions.

Phoebe Astley looked at Coffin. 'I guess this is what you wanted to provoke, sir?'

'In part, Phoebe. I always want more than I get.'

Then DC Parsons, in charge of Board E, stood up. 'Sir, I am getting stories that you were meant to be the victim in the church shooting.'

Coffin said that he had heard that story too; it was possible. He was always likely to be a victim of a man with a gun.

'Or a woman,' muttered Phoebe. 'Don't let's forget women. You mentioned women at first. Keep it up. We can shoot.'

'You mean you think it could be true,' said a voice from the floor. 'That you were meant to be the victim?'

Coffin said yes, he was willing to be *a* victim. Even *the* victim, but it looked as though this killer was spreading the role around.

'Could anyone be a victim?' said the same voice. It was Grahame Godley. 'Or was there a certain sort of victim?'

'I think it's anyone who comes in handy,' said someone who hadn't spoken before, a tall man called James Whitley, part of the team working on Dr Murray's murder. Uninvited officers were creeping in as opportunity offered. No one wanted to be left out of what was exceedingly important.

'No, I can't accept that,' said Annie Bertram. 'The children's bus must have been followed and so must the Chief Commander's car. No, no chance.'

'The choice of victims must have some point,' said Phoebe Astley. She wanted this to be so because it would make finding the killer easier: find the reason for the killing and you are halfway there.

That was her view anyway, and she got a mutter of agreement from her colleagues. There were rules about killing, sometimes broken, but more consistent than murderers thought because the killer believed he was unique.

'What are the motives?' Phoebe said, standing up so she could be heard and staring into faces to see what reaction she got.

Anger . . . really vicious, physical rage.

Jealousy.

Mental trouble of some sort.

Fear. Potent as a motive, this.

Money . . . killers could be paid.

'Have I missed one out?' she asked.

'No.' Coffin knew she was saying all this to see what she would get back from her audience. 'I think that list covers it.'

'Did you get what you want?' asked Stella, who had regarded his meeting with the eye of a theatrical producer.

'Some interesting questions came up. You could say I banged their heads together.'

They were enjoying a before-dinner drink, if enjoy was the word when Stella was checking a play script and Coffin was drawing several large packets from his briefcase.

'I ought to have given you a trunk not a briefcase for your birthday,' said Stella, observing the load he had been carrying around. The elegant case she had chosen had been distorted out of shape by the burden pressed inside it. 'Did you have to bring all that home?' Even Stella recognized that this was a very wifely remark. She blamed the Jacobean-style drama she was reading called *Did the Wife Do It?*

'Yes, good old Phoebe,' said Coffin absently.

Maybe I should be jealous of Phoebe, thought Stella, returning to her play. But no, a woman who can wear shoes such as she does, with legs like hers, needs help not envy. She looked down with approval at her own neat Prada sandals. Well, I haven't the least idea what we shall eat for dinner tonight, and that'll teach him.

Down below the bell rang on the front door, a loud but delicate chime.

Coffin looked up. 'Oh, I forgot to say that I ordered a meal from the restaurant. I knew you were busy, and I knew I was, but we must eat.'

'Do you order it, or did Phoebe?'

'I didn't even hear that.'

Stella folded the script and threw it at him, just missing.

Coffin picked up the script, smoothed it straight. 'Well named,' he said. 'I think the wife did do it . . . I will go to collect the meal.'

He took in the tray; the meal had been arranged on it by Alfredo, who was running the restaurants (there were three now) while his father was in Italy. In spite of their Italian names and pride in their Milanese ancestry, they were South Londoners from generations back.

'Thanks.' He passed over payment plus a good tip. 'How's your dad?'

'He's having a good holiday and trying to learn Italian.'

Coffin raised an eyebrow.

'Yes, I know he always pretends we speak nothing else at home. Not true. We speak English.'

Alfredo spoke beautiful English; he was clever and in his final year at one of the better local universities. His chosen subject, as Coffin knew, was mathematics. 'That's my language,' he had said.

Stella knows about faces, he thought, as they ate the chicken and salad. I'll ask her. 'Stella, if you could spare the time, would you look at some photographs with me?'

She reached out and took one. 'That's one of the Jackson girls.' Her face was pale and her eyes puckered. 'I know it is one of them, but I can't recognize which one. The face is changed.'

'Violent death does that to the face,' said Coffin. And the girl had been dead some time when this photograph was taken, but he thought he wouldn't tell Stella. The dead girl was Alice Jackson. He had an idea that Stella had liked Alice a good deal; he also thought that Stella was looking at Alice's battered and slightly decayed face with fear but could not admit it.

He did not let her see the photograph of her twin Amy because it was, on the whole, worse. He did not care to dwell on it himself. There was something that disturbed and worried him.

The picture of Mrs Jackson herself showed her face down, as if she had been hit from behind, which was thought to be the case. The girls had looked at their killer, known what was coming.

The rolled-up overall that Mrs Jackson had worn at work in the hospital was by her side and caught some of the blood. It seemed as though she had just come in from work when she was attacked. She might even have let her killer into the house, innocently walking in front of him. If it was a him.

'I'll do my best for you, Mrs Jackson,' Coffin heard himself mutter under his breath, so that Stella looked at him in surprise.

'I'll take my things upstairs to work.'

Once it had been the favoured hidey-hole of dear, sick Gus, always crouching on the window sill, ready to bark at the passing cat on the roof. Coffin missed his bark, and often felt like doing his own barking up there. He felt he could do with Gus's astringent but soothing company; he didn't like the affair he was into.

He took the file of Jack Jackson next because of the relationship with the rest of the family, although Dr Murray had been the next victim. He didn't expect to get much there, nor did he. The file held no revelation. From the angle at which he had been shot, it was probable he had seen his killer, whom he might have known.

'I bet he did know him,' said Coffin to himself. 'Got that feeling.' Still, he had been in the Force long enough to distrust feelings.

Dr Murray came next. There were several photographs

here of that strange and gruesome death. He spread the photographs in a circle on the table in front of him.

There was the body of Dr Murray with the tiny infant skulls arranged above her. Hard to see the point of this, but there had to be one. It aroused memories in his mind of the pit where the Neanderthal skulls had been found.

Did this mean that the killer of Dr Murray had also seen those skulls? The killer had certainly seen Dr Murray's interest in these skulls in the museum, of this Coffin was certain. Had the gold ring come from there? Coffin knew enough about the Neanderthals, who co-existed with modern man for some time, to know that they were not ape men, and could work metal, possibly gold. So Dr Murray might have extracted it from the museum to investigate it. There were no modern markings on it.

The killer knew about the Neanderthals, Coffin decided, even if he had not seen them. Or she had not seen them; about the sex of the killer he was still keeping an open mind. He sensed a female presence, somehow. Now why was that?

Because of the children's heads, he supposed. Babies, mothers, they came together. Reminded him of the Walkers Club.

Blood too, a lot of blood in childbirth. With his forefinger he traced the shape of the big bloodstain in the photograph. It was a lot of blood, and you had to remember that there were two lots of blood: Dr Murray's and one other, which was HIV positive. Was this sickness powering the killer's fury? There was anger here.

Coffin studied one of the larger photographs, which took in the circle of skulls, the display of bones and skulls in the cupboards behind, as well as the window, which seemed to give on to an interior corridor. A few onlookers seemed to have collected there too, pressing against the glass to see what they could see.

Coffin walked to the window of his own room to look out at the dark sky, which he found soothing.

What was Dr Murray doing in the museum anyway? he

asked himself as he walked back to his desk. To look at the heads, came the answer. They were all deformed, as was the single more modern head found in the Neanderthal pit.

Did the killer follow her there, or find her there, or did she take the killer in with her?

Chance or planning, he went for planning every time.

There was no photograph of dead or maimed children from the school bus, because none had been harmed. Thank God for that, he thought. No one was hurt.

He heard a creak and for a moment he thought it was Gus. Gus back home from the clinic, the only dog with a triple bypass. Could be triple hearts, he thought, with the bills he was paying. Come home soon, Gus. He had a bell on his collar and Coffin thought he could hear that bell distantly now. Certainly something.

It was the new cat, pushing open the door. She had come on a lot with good food and a happy life. She was happy, you could see it in her eyes.

'You'd better like Gus,' he said stroking her head. 'And make him like you, because Gus was mighty fond of the old moggie.'

The next set of photographs was of Lia and her children. No heads, no connection with Neanderthals. He knew the name of her husband, though; his criminal past had long been known to him.

'I never nicked him,' Coffin said to himself. 'Not what a Chief Commander does, but I certainly knew his name.'

Stella came to the bottom of the stairs to call up. 'Want some coffee?'

'Yes, please. Shall I come down?'

'No, I'll come up.' She was already on the way. 'How are you?'

'Just thinking.'

'Painful, is it?'

'Not more than usually,' he said with a sigh. He accepted the coffee, which was hot and strong. 'This ought to keep my mind ticking over.'

'My idea.'

He gave her a shrewd look. 'You didn't just come up with the coffee to make me happy?'

'No, Phoebe rang . . . You didn't answer the phone so I took the call.'

'I didn't hear it, must be getting deaf.'

'No, just concentrating . . . I've noticed it.'

Coffin groaned. 'Tell me the worst.'

'It's the Lumsdens.'

'Oh God, what's happened there?'

'Lumsden himself rang in. Said they were together. Apologized for going off as he had. He will be taking a bit of leave so they can have a second honeymoon.'

'I suppose that's good news,' said Coffin doubtfully.

'Do you believe it? I wasn't sure if Phoebe did.'

'Phoebe's not one for the romantic ending.'

'No,' said Stella thoughtfully. 'She wouldn't be.'

'Time will tell . . . Either they will both come back or two bodies will turn up.'

Coffin went back to Lia Boston. The photographs here were an unpleasant testimony to the ruthlessness of the killer: Lia had tried to protect her children with her own body and failed. The forensic scientist whose report was attached suggested that Lia had thrown herself across the children and been dragged aside.

She was killed first. What was the evidence for this? Firstly the tears on the sleeves of her dress, as if they been grabbed and wrenched, and secondly the bruises on her shoulders and neck. She had died first. At least one of the children, a boy, had taken some time to die.

He didn't want to look into the faces of the dead children, but he forced himself to do so. The killer had spared the childish features by shooting through the neck so that one lay with eyes closed apparently in peaceful sleep, provided you could ignore a great tear in the throat. Next to the sleeper, the boy with curly hair had his eyes and mouth open, caught in terror. The face of the other child was so covered in blood from Lia, which had dripped all over the place, that there was no chance for any expression to be seen.

Last of all, but as yet no photographs for him to look at, was his very own incident. The shooting at the christening.

Coffin leant back in his chair, shuffling through the photographs. An idea was beginning to take shape, but dimly, only dimly.

He picked up the file of notes to begin studying them. He began, as seemed right, with Mrs Jackson.

She was a nurse, in charge of a team working in the maternity block, and the mother of two beautiful daughters, both of whom Stella Pinero knew.

Jack Jackson was the son, much older than the two girls, and a different character altogether: a handsome rogue, a devilish crook, a killer in the making . . . it all depended how you felt about him. Trust him you couldn't, like him you sometimes found yourself doing, willy-nilly. A clever man, Jack, and Coffin thought he had been attacked because he guessed who had killed his mother. He had survived for some time, just about alive, with a police guard, only to die wordlessly.

Since Coffin was beginning to make a guess himself, he had to hope he would not be killed.

Then he thought: but someone did have a pop at me. Or did they? Perhaps the bullet was meant for Marie Rudkin.

Considering the Jackson file, he thought the later killings had made Inspector Lavender's idea that someone just walked in and did the job less likely.

He moved on to the killing of Dr Murray. Phoebe Astley herself, assisted by Inspector Dover, had been investigating here. She was always careful and meticulous.

The circle of children's heads had interested her. There had to be some point, she argued. Following Sergeant Ash's initial interview, Phoebe had re-interviewed the husband, cousin and cousin's husband. 'They are in a bad way there,' she had written on the report. 'Don't know why. I think another look might be useful.'

Coffin thought he would go himself.

He opened the file on Lia Boston. Some more coffee would be useful here. Inspector Dover was famous for his dull reports. He was, however, as meticulous as Phoebe Astley, although without her flair.

The husband, a well-known local criminal, was being met at Heathrow. Lia's mother lived in Newcastle; they were not close and she would not be coming south. Lia had no siblings.

Careful as ever, Dover had identified and interviewed a couple of her friends: Letty Brown and Sheila Fish. Lia had hinted to them that she had knowledge – as did her husband – about the run of murders by shooting. Both young women were adamant that they themselves knew nothing. In fact, they had not believed that Lia herself did.

'She could tell a tale,' Sheila had said. 'And we weren't that close. We just knew each other because we had babies at the same time in the same hospital. But we used to go for walks together, pushing the babies in the prams, because it can be boring walking on your own. Then once a week or so we would meet for coffee. The Walkers Club, we called it.'

DI Dover had enclosed a transcript of his questioning of the two women.

He would be questioning the husband.

A possible breakthrough, thought Coffin, closing his eyes so he could think the better. He had made up his mind that he would be interviewing all the families concerned.

'I'm better at asking the right questions,' he said aloud.

Children, babies, seemed to crop up all the time. That's the motif, he said to himself dreamily, like a repeated decorative phrase in a piece of music.

The cat slid down from its perch near the window to settle in comfort on the desk. The file of papers made a good nest, if you moved them round a bit, which she did not hesitate to do. She had known for some time now that she was an established figure and no longer on sufferance. The cat of the house.

*   *   *

Stella finished reading the script, made her notes on it, then put the work away. She climbed the stairs to Coffin's workroom.

She stood at the door, looking at him. He had fallen asleep at the desk, his head on the folder he had been using last, almost nose to nose with the cat. They breathed in unison.

'You're worn out, you poor darling.' Her voice was soft. 'You've had a tough day. It's a rough old world.' She touched his head, smoothing the dark hair. 'Tomorrow will be better.'

Neither of them knew of the critical forces then massing for the attack on Coffin.

11

Not a day Coffin wants to remember.

Inspector Larry Lavender looked around the room at the back of the bar in the Leaping Lady pub with some satisfaction. He thought he had arranged things well: in the first place he always liked the Leaping Lady, which went alliteratively with his own name and pleased him, and in the second place this back room was cosy. Comfortable, cheerful and clean. There it was again, that pleasing alliteration.

'Come in, Ken,' he said cheerfully. 'I've got the drinks in.'

DS Ken Ireland nodded without speaking. He had already worked out that this was a time to keep quiet and say little. A swift look round the room to check if they would be taped left the question open.

Larry Lavender wore his usual dark unobtrusive suit with the tie that had a vaguely military air, dark with a stripe, as if he had been in the Guards and marched up and down outside Windsor Castle. The rest of the room were following the latest fashion of no tie and unbuttoned neck in a sporty-looking shirt.

'Ah, there you are, Jim.' DS Jim Ward admitted he was there, his eye on the table, which was loaded in a hospitable way with bottles. Too much to hope for a whisky.

Others were filing in behind him, all pretty punctual. Somehow Larry Lavender was not someone you kept waiting. He knew most of the faces, Geoff Little, Grahame Godley, and there was DS Annie Bertram. Ward edged towards her; he was hoping to make his way with her. Probably not, she was said to be canny and cautious, but on the other hand there was something about her bottom and the way she walked that attracted him mightily.

Annie Bertram had seen him looking at her, and knew exactly which bit of her he fancied and what he hoped to do about it. He had told DS Eric Foster, strictly in confidence, of course, who had told DC Lenny Armstrong, who had passed it on as a strictly private bit of news to WDC Flip Armitage, who had at once told Annie. For that matter, Annie had heard a joke about it in the canteen. Ward's chances with her were minimal . . . On the other hand, there was something about him.

She brushed past him as she moved towards the table to take a beer. Yes, good hair and nice cologne, but he'd have to work harder to get anywhere with her. And learn not to have too many best friends to talk to.

The room was filling up. She did not recognize all the faces but she could see that they represented a good selection of the more successful serving CID officers of the Second City.

'Well, I'm a lucky girl to be here then,' she told herself. On the other hand she could see that Paul Masters was not here, nor CI Phoebe Astley, nor, although lower down the scale, was Tony Davley, whom she counted as a friend.

There were warning signs in that list.

Larry Lavender was skilful at organizing a party, and now he drew them all into a group. Fairly close in, because he did not wish to shout.

'You must all be wondering what this is all about.'

'Larry,' said a voice from the back, 'we are detectives . . . grant us that much.' It was Geoff Little, drinking his beer but keeping his eye on the door. He wanted to know who came in and went out. The early departures might carry their own message . . . like a vote in the House of Commons. His cousin had just got into Parliament for a marginal seat at the last general election, and he felt he knew how politics worked.

'That's what this is about: every man,' he cast a quick look round, 'and woman too, is a highly professional detective. We are at good at what we do. Forgive me if I am talking at you like a doctor or a college lecturer . . .'

'No,' said a voice, not Geoff Little this time, but a detective sergeant from the outer limits of the Second City. 'Get on with it, Larry, I've got a date to keep.'

'Right, this is it: we've each of us been doing a damn good job on this serial gunman we've got. All right, we haven't caught him yet.'

'But we will.' This time it was Frank Fielder, working on the Jackson case. One of the Jackson cases. 'If we don't get too much help from above . . .'

'You call it help?' There was a murmur, no more than an echo in the room.

'It's better too, isn't it?'

'I don't know about that,' said Larry, 'but what I know is I want to be allowed to do my job in my own way.'

Into the silence that followed, he said, 'Now you know why we are here. I thought we would all meet here to talk it over.' His voice was gentle.

'You could call it a protest meeting,' said a voice.

It's insubordination, thought Geoff Little, it's insurrection, it might be a revolution. Not the French Revolution, because that began on the streets, but the Russian Revolution, put together by a devious and clever mind. Lenin Larry Lavender, step forward. Little was doing a degree in historical studies with the Open University. He had said once that if you were just a copper there was no hope for you; you had to make something else of yourself, even if it was only bee-keeping. Joke. See Sherlock Holmes.

Larry Lavender was speaking again, his voice ever more gentle. 'In several of the most recent important cases, the Chief Commander has come in and interfered. Now we know he is moving into this serial killer. We don't want that, do we?'

He might have been moving a vote of thanks.

That was the thing about old Larry, thought Little, who had worked with him once or twice, he could make the direct threat sound like an invitation to the vicar's tea party. Because it was a threat to John Coffin. And to everyone in that room, if it failed.

He couldn't make up his mind whether to run for the door or stay there. But his legs would not move.

12

Monday. The days get blurred.

What remained of the Walkers held a small sad meeting in
Letty's house to talk about the death of Lia. Letty's house was
a good meeting place, because it was in central Spinnergate,
on a quiet side road. Letty's house was decorated by her
husband, who liked being a good houseman, so the paint was
always fresh and the wallpaper new. He liked strong colours,
so visitors sometimes blinked at the vivid blues and orange
reds. Perhaps on this account, Letty usually entertained in
the kitchen, over whose colour scheme she had had control;
it was white and pale grey. She made good coffee and offered
homemade shortbread.

Even Natty came this time, apologizing for being absent so
often. Unlike the other two, she looked tired and untidy, in
pale blue jeans and a dark shirt.

No one wears jeans now, not this season, not that colour
or shape, Letty thought. And she might have combed her
hair.

'Oh we understand, love,' said Sheila. 'Of course we do.'

'And I hadn't got a pram to push,' said Natty sadly. 'Well,
I've got the pram. I never sold it, but it's empty.'

'Perhaps not for ever,' said Sheila.

'I think so. You can't fight the gods.'

Sheila thought you could if you chose. 'Depends which god
you are talking to.'

'Oh, talking,' said Natty. 'What about Lia, she was a talker

153

and look what's happened to her . . . What did she say, by the way?'

Sheila shrugged. 'Not much, just hints of what she said her husband had told her. But she always did exaggerate. And he's such a liar too, anyway, we told her that, or we tried to.' Had they? She couldn't now remember. She certainly had thought Lia's husband was a stranger to the truth, and often claimed knowledge he did not have. Look at the time he had spread the story that he had joined the Montjoy gang as the electronics expert and they had raided the Bank of England but it had been kept quiet, hushed up, because the authorities were ashamed. A fool if you believed that, but many did.

Letty came in with a jug of coffee and a plate of chocolate biscuits, not homemade this time. To please her husband she was wearing a tight orange-red skirt, but to please herself she was wearing a crisp white shirt. 'I know we are all on diets but choccie biccies are cheering and we need cheering up. I'm terrified as well as miserable. How are you?'

'I think a strong gin might help me more than coffee,' said Sheila. 'Letty, that skirt makes me blink.' She herself had on a blue and white jersey dress. Neat and not conspicuous.

Letty was ever practical. 'We can have that afterwards.' She passed over the comment on her skirt.

'Good job you're not still feeding the kid,' said Natasha.

'Lord no, that's long past. Just as well, ruins the figure.' She drank her coffee. 'Nice to see you, Nat. How are you?'

'Lousy,' said Nat. 'This is a bloody business.' She took a deep breath, then, 'And with my cousin being killed too . . .'

Letty and Sheila exchanged glances. Although they had discussed it already, they did not know what to say, or whether to say anything. Natasha was never easy to read, sometimes lively and witty, at other times morose.

'She has secrets, that girl,' Sheila had said.

'Don't we all?' Letty had answered. 'I've got a few, and I bet you have.'

'I think it's gin time,' said Letty, producing a bottle. 'Or whisky. I believe there is some if my husband hasn't drunk

154

it all. He doesn't drink gin, calls it a woman's drink.' She was prattling on, anxious to keep the mood light. Jolly they could not be, since this was, in a sense, a wake. 'So choose, gin or whisky, friends.'

Natty took a good long drink of gin and lemon. 'I think I know why my cousin went to look in the museum of old bones.'

Letty coughed.

'Oh well, you know what I mean . . . part of the forensic outfit in the hospital, its skulls of interest. My cousin knew it, but no one went there much. Science is different now.'

'Is it?' asked Sheila.

'She said so. It's true not many people bothered with it. Yet she went there . . . So why?'

'You'll never know, will you?' said Letty solemnly; the gin was getting to her too.

'I met her with the car, as I very often met her from work . . . I used to help her out all the time . . . kind of like a secretary, chauffeur and homehelp combined. She was rich, richish anyway, and we weren't. Anyway, she left me a legacy, but naturally most of her money has gone to her husband . . .'

Letty began to wonder if she had been wise to pour out the gin. I gave her too much, she thought. She's had a bad time, her cousin and everything; she's disturbed.

'She had seen the deposit of infant skulls just uncovered . . . Chief Commander John Coffin was there too. She told him they were infant Neanderthal skulls, decapitated babies, probably sacrificial victims, the flesh eaten.'

Letty swallowed hard.

'I don't think he liked the idea . . .'

'Nice man,' said Sheila soothingly.

'I think that's what took her to the museum . . . she wanted to check up on something.'

'Perhaps she thought there was a colony of Neanderthals living near here . . . There is Nean Street, isn't there?'

She is drunk, thought Letty. I overdid it there.

'Little short men with big hands.'

'I expect there's some of them about.' She wanted to add that they would be harmless, but she couldn't quite say so, because who knew? She saw such a specimen doing his shopping at irregular hours and she believed he lived in Nean Street, so if anyone could be called a modern-day Neanderthal it would be him. But surely a man who did his own shopping and bought frozen fish pie must be harmless?

'Poor Lia did mix with a bad crowd, thanks to Boston,' said Sheila. 'The police must be looking at her husband.'

'He'd never kill his own children.'

'You just can't tell.'

Letty tried to decide whether to offer more coffee or more gin, but Nat stood up and said she must go. 'I do have a husband, and I'm even looking after my cousin's husband too. We go round every day, or he comes to us. And of course, the police keep coming around asking us all the questions they can think of.'

'We've had a bit of that too,' said Letty. 'Haven't we, Sheila? It looks as though we were the last people to see her, so naturally the police keep thinking about us. I wouldn't say they suspect us, but they certainly think we could help them. "Who are her friends? What people was she in contact with?" That sort of thing . . . I suppose they think if they ask often enough we might come up with something.'

'I thought I might go into the church round the corner and say a prayer for Lia and light a candle,' said Sheila.

'She's past all that,' said Natty, sadly. She kissed each cheek. 'End of the Walkers.' They were all part of it, the Walkers.

'Fraid so,' said Letty. 'Already over really, anyway, wasn't it? But fun while it lasted.'

'Over for me before it began,' said Natty.

When she had gone, the other two looked at each other. 'I'm glad we've got our kids, aren't you?' said Letty. 'Makes even having a husband worthwhile.'

Then they both began to laugh and advise each other to have some more gin.

This was their little holiday, their morning off. Sheila had taken her two children to a nursery school in Spinnergate and Letty had got her mother to look after hers. 'Can't afford the nursery school. Wish I could.'

'Neither can I,' said Sheila, 'but I told my husband that if he didn't do something about it, I would go mad. Since he didn't want a mad wife, he agreed. They only go twice a week, but it's enough.' She had been an extremely efficient computer expert and hankered to go back, but she had given it up to look after the recalcitrant babies.

'You'll go back,' Letty assured her. She had not been so high-powered herself, and had no hankering to go back to selling bras and pants.

'In that business,' said the computer whizz kid gravely, 'you get out of date so soon. I'd have to be reborn almost.'

Letty felt it would not be past her.

'I wish we could have helped Lia.'

'She had plenty of money.'

'Crook money.'

'Maybe.'

'And it killed her in the end. Anyway, that's what I think, but who cares, no one will ask me for my opinion.'

'I don't know about that,' said Letty gravely.

Sheila studied her face; this was not the gin talking. 'You know something I don't?'

Letty lowered her eyes. 'My sister-in-law works in the Chief Commander's office. Only the outer office, you understand, but she's in charge of the telephones and the faxes . . . She told me that the Chief Commander is very worried. He's taking charge himself and will be interviewing all friends and contacts.'

'Us,' said Sheila.

They drank a little more gin, then Sheila put down her glass with decision. 'Let's go and light that candle for Lia.'

'And say a prayer?'

'Yes,' said Sheila seriously. 'That must come first. Can't do one without the other.'

The church across the road was small, dark, quiet and empty. No parson, no other worshippers, but there were some candles.

'You've been here before,' Letty accused.

'Yes, I often pop in. I find it helps.'

'I wish it was easy as that for me,' said Letty.

'Oh, it's not easy. Doesn't come automatically, like eating chocolate.'

'No?' Strange comparison, Letty thought.

'You have to work at it.' Sheila bought them each a candle, handed one to Letty and lit both, since Letty was strangely clumsy.

'We ought to say a prayer for ourselves too,' she said softly.

'Yes, if you think so.' Letty was doubtful, but willing. 'But we're outside it all, aren't we?'

'I'm not so sure,' said Sheila. 'Bad crimes have a kind of a circumference. Make a circle. And I think we are inside.'

'And I think you are frightening me.'

'Not on purpose.' She added, 'Brian would agree with me if I talked about it to him.'

'Brian?' said Letty absently.

'My husband.'

'Oh, yes, of course – it's just that you usually call him Bri.'

'Not when I'm talking seriously. He knows then I'm in earnest. Don't you have words like that?'

Letty thought about it. 'No.'

Brian was an ambitious young man on his way up; she wasn't sure what he worked at, but it was something in advertising, and he probably did need two languages. Her own husband taught in a large comprehensive school in the Second City, where he said that life was a fight for survival. He did survive though, and on a visit to a school concert Letty had observed that he was on good terms with his pupils, whom he clearly liked. Not such a bad life after all, she had decided.

'And anyway,' said Sheila with resolution, 'we aren't outside it, not with Natty's cousin being killed and now Lia.'

'But that's just coincidence.' Letty tried to sound cold and intellectual about it. 'These serial killers just go for who's handy.'

'Nothing personal, you mean?' Sheila was sceptical.

'Nothing personal,' said Letty dolefully.

'God, I hope not,' said Sheila.

Natasha had been glad to escape from the Walkers' party. As she left the house she had sighted another former Walker, pushing her pram, but not in the direction of Letty's home. An ex-Walker, then.

Innocent of us, really, to think that once we'd had the babies we'd be able to keep up the same comradeship, she thought. Not that I ever got the chance to find out, she added to herself with a shrug.

She gave Maisie (it was Maisie?) a wave and hurried on. Trailing along with her, like one of those fashionable pashminas that every one was wearing a summer ago, came misery. It hung from her shoulders, sagged near her waist, then went off to drape her feet. Misery made breathing and walking difficult.

In the distance she could see the roof of the hospital building where Dr Murray's body had been found, certified dead, and then investigated in the post-mortem.

Oh coz, how could you be a victim? You didn't act like a victim, you didn't talk like a victim. Added to which, she added with a bitter humour that surprised her, you paid a large part of my wages.

A mixture of wrath and repentence rose in her throat so that she had to lean towards the gutter to be sick.

'Drunken whore,' said an old man, as he hobbled past.

'Fuck yourself,' said Nat, lifting her head to glare at him. 'No one else will.' But since she was still vomiting, if he heard it was no more than a mutter. He had a bony, red-skinned face with a large nose.

She straightened up. She felt better and realized that the sickness and the words had been a joint act of cleansing.

She passed the tube station and looked at it longingly. A trip to central London would be so refreshing, purging almost, but she must get back to her own household. In it she had two men in need of her support, one her own husband and the other the widower of Margaret Murray.

There was a big poster advertising Stella Pinero in her latest production at the St Luke's Theatre on the hoarding by the Spinnergate tube: *The Jasmine Summer*.

Lucky thing, thought Natty, she's got everything.

Mimsie Marker saw Natasha walk past. She knew who she was because she knew everyone of interest, which Natasha was at the moment, since her cousin's murder.

Stella Pinero had just bought a paper from Mimsie to read on the underground journey to London. She had disappeared down the escalator, even as Natasha passed by.

Mimsie frowned. One of her informants had told her something that would worry Stella if she knew. Perhaps she did know, but her informant had told her that not even the Chief Commander knew. 'Buzzing around him like a lot of wasps,' the informant had said.

Stella Pinero also had her informants. It pays in show business to know all the gossip. This particular buzz had been passed to her by a girl who worked in the hair, wigs and makeup department at the theatre. It had not come directly but Edwina (christened Edna, but you don't stay with a name like that if you work in the theatre) had filtered the tale through Stella's secretary, a woman adept at passing on whatever she thought Stella ought to know. About this tale she had hesitated, since it was not theatre gossip although certainly doing the rounds.

'Like wasps,' she said to Stella as she finished.

'You can drive me to the station,' was all Stella said. 'Never anywhere to park there.' But she muttered her thanks as she got on the escalator, well aware that the Eyes and Ears of the Second City in the shape of Mimsie Marker had observed her. Apologetically, she added, 'I know, these murders are terrible; I was fond of Alice Jackson, and Amy too.'

'Buzzing round,' she muttered resentfully as she went down and down, clinging on to the escalator rail: Her purpose in going to the other London, to Knightsbridge, was to discuss with the designer the costumes for her next project for millennium year: *The Widow of Windsor*.

'A musical of all things. How have I got the courage?' thought Stella as she got out of the train, having changed lines twice. She could have taken a taxi but she was in a determinedly frugal mood. Since she was going to spend so much money on a show that might lose a great deal (and Coffin had raised his eyebrows sceptically when it was projected, which made Stella even more resolute for success), economy had to be practised elsewhere.

She cast a guilty look at her new Prada suit, but that was last week. From now on she would be very economical. The thing about good clothes, she affirmed, with the conviction of the true fashion addict, was that they Supported the Spirit, so they were never Money Wasted.

The designer, Edward Crowne, whom she was about to see, was a well-known couturier who had been chosen for his name and fame, and also because the real work would be done by his assistant, Emily Woodhouse, who was very talented.

After greeting Edward Crowne, Stella retired to another room to look at Emily's sketches.

'Brilliant, Emily, I knew they would be.'

'Come and have lunch with me, and we can talk.'

'I would love to, Emily, but I must get back.'

'I understand . . . you're having a bad time in the Second City.'

'Won't do the theatre any good. Nothing like a serial killer to put people off a night at a show,' said Stella trying to make light of it. 'It's worse for my husband.'

'Must be. Look, if there's anything I can do, if you want a hole to hide in at any time, you can always stay with me.'

'Thank you, Emily.' Stella managed her first smile of the day. She thought that Phoebe Astley, in one of those offbeat moods she went in for, or was reputed to go in for, might be a better invitee, but it was nice to be found attractive, even if just as one on Emily's list.

Emily looked at her and laughed. 'Okay, Stella, we understand each other. I was just asking. I thought you seemed a bit off the distinguished copper.'

Back in the Second City, Stella went first to the theatre to hand over the folder of designs to her producer.

'Swatches of silks and cottons are attached to each design, so you will see what you are getting.'

Fred Fuser touched the silks with a loving forefinger. 'Beautiful stuff . . . I am going to enjoy working with the costumes.'

'I may have to cut a few corners.'

'Not too many,' said Fred earnestly. 'Quality counts. A soprano sings better in a good silk. I've seen it, heard it, no joke.'

'You never joke, Fred,' said Stella as she departed to see Marie. 'I'm off to the University Hospital.' She had been transferred from St Thomas's.

'You're not ill?' He was alarmed. His professional life was bound up with Stella's. He was going to go far, he knew it, but he needed this production of a big musical this millennium year.

But she was gone.

Stella found Marie Rudkin propped up on pillows, her face white, but her eyes open. She looked pleased to see Stella.

Stella took the hand that lay on the sheet. 'This is the first time the nurses have let me in. I have tried before.'

'I know. And you have telephoned every day. They let me know, even if I wasn't allowed to do anything about it.'

Stella sat down by the side of the bed. 'I haven't brought any flowers,' she said apologetically. She looked around the room; no flowers at all.

'I don't like them. They make me sneeze, and a sneeze is painful when you have a hole in your chest.' Cheerfully, she added, 'Better me than the baby.'

'My husband thinks the bullet was meant for him.'

Marie was quiet. Then she said, 'It could have been. But I think it was for me. But perhaps the attacker didn't mind who he hit. If he had to hit someone, perhaps I was the best one to get.'

'I don't suppose your husband thinks that.'

'If it wasn't painful laughing, I would laugh. No, he wishes it was him, but that's rubbish, of course. He couldn't be spared.'

Marie paused for a moment, then she said slowly, 'I saw the man who shot me, I remember that, but I cannot remember his face.

'Not yet. But I think I will remember . . . it's there at the back of my mind. The curtain will lift.'

John Coffin listened to Paul Masters and Phoebe Astley give an account of Larry Lavender's meeting. They had not attended but they seemed very well informed about it.

'Buzzing about like wasps?' He laughed, but the melancholy inside him since he had set up the Crime Forum, getting the reports from forensics and weaponry, who seemed to have nothing helpful to say on the serial shooter, did not lift. 'Or is it fleas?'

He leant back in his chair. His desk was piled with papers he must read, and any moment the telephone might ring, but he wanted to hear this. He hadn't decided yet whether to be amused or angry, but any moment a strong feeling one way or the other would rush over him and he would know. One bit of good news had been handed to him, unconnected with the murders – a card from the missing Constable Lumsden to the chief of his station to say that he and his wife were touring the Highlands and the dog was with them. He didn't have much interest in Lumsden, but anything was better just now than a missing constable who might have murdered his wife. And dog. The great British public would probably mind most about the dog.

'Fleas don't buzz,' said Phoebe.

'No, they crawl around silently till you scratch. Well, thanks for not joining the crawlers.'

'We weren't asked.'

'Ah.'

'Larry knew we would tell you,' said Paul.

'We had our spies there, though,' Phoebe nodded.

'One inside and one out.' This was Paul.

'You're enjoying this,' said Coffin. They were on his side, but there was a secret pleasure at finding him being buzzed.

'The meeting was in a pub, after all, a private back room, but with a hatch opening on the middle room. Anyone leaning against it could hear everything.'

'And who was?'

'I was, sir,' said Paul Masters. 'Good beer they serve there.'

'If you like beer,' said Phoebe. 'I go for vodka or gin myself.' She was in a very good, bouncy mood.

'And who was inside?' Coffin wondered what had brought this about with her.

'CI Alec Gidding from Tutton Street Division.'

'Oh yes, I know him, of course.' Gidding was always willing to shout his mouth off and be angry, although his anger never extended to his happy married life and the donkey sanctuary he helped run in Leppard Street on the river side. Coffin respected him for that.

'Larry invited him. Angry man and all that, but he doesn't like Larry. He says Larry once trod on one of his donkey's tails and didn't say sorry.'

'I'm not sure if I've ever believed that tale,' said Coffin.

'No, well, it may not be true but it makes a good story, and he doesn't like Larry but Larry doesn't know it.'

'So he was invited to the meeting?'

'Yes, and Alec came to me. He does like me; I have never trodden on a donkey's tail.'

Coffin looked at his watch. 'Nearly time for something to eat ... Stella left home early to go to London, I think we missed breakfast out.'

'What about the cat?' asked Phoebe, still oddly the cat's protector.

'No, the cat has eaten,' said Coffin kindly. 'Biscuits, fish and milk. Stella left it ready, but I didn't fancy joining her. Let's go to the Leaping Lady.'

'You did know about this meeting?' accused Phoebe.

'We can walk, can't we? Just around the corner.'

'Several corners,' said Paul Masters. 'Any good asking how you knew about the meeting, sir?'

Coffin laughed. 'I am a detective, or I like to think I am. Larry Lavender left too many clues. Perhaps he meant to. Not much good organizing an insurrection if the victim doesn't know.'

'That's very cynical, sir.'

'I picked up the feeling at the meeting of the Crime Forum.'

A good idea with dangerous implications. In retrospect he could see that he had brought together a group of people who resented his ways.

I've only just grasped it, he thought, as they plodded round to the Leaping Lady (which was by no means round the corner and it had begun to rain). This pair have known for some time. It's not liked when I act as a detective and not the head of the Force. Perhaps they even feel the same, but they're too decent to show it.

'Sorry you're getting wet,' he said to Phoebe.

'That's all right, sir, not very wet; it's only just damping down and we're almost there.'

'You're bloody loyal.' And he wished passionately that Stella was with him.

'Yes sir,'

The lights of the Leaping Lady shone through the rain. 'This place used to be called the Heart of Oak,' Coffin said. 'And don't ask what that meant, probably one of Nelson's battleships. Full of the past down here. I dare say there's a memorial to King Canute if we ask about it.'

The drinkers in the bar, all smartly dressed men and women of the new City, bankers, brokers, accountants, looked as if they would ask if Canute was a new pop group.

There was an empty table in one corner of the room, to which Coffin led the way. As soon as they were seated (and just three comfortable seats as Phoebe noted), the landlord hurried over with a tray. A large vodka and two large whiskies were planted on the table with a smile. 'Here you are, sir.' Then he bustled off, still smiling.

'He knew we were coming,' said Phoebe, still accusatory.

Straight-faced, Coffin said, 'It's the first task of any detective when he comes to a new area to set up his network. Dick here has always been on mine. And as it happens I knew him when we walked the beat together back in Deptford.'

'So that's how you knew about Larry Lavender's game,' said Paul.

'One of the ways.' Coffin drank some whisky. 'There might be others.'

Phoebe sipped her vodka, which was excellent and she was an expert at quality. This was one of the occasions when she never quite knew if the Chief Commander was playing a game of his own with her or telling the straight truth. A mixture of both, likely enough. She was glad to see some of the strain had lifted from his eyes.

She took a quick look at herself in the big looking-glass on the wall in front and decided that with a little more vodka it would have gone from her eyes too.

Paul Masters, also reflected in the glass and looking back at her, was wearing dark spectacles, which was as good a way of hiding as any.

'I know I irritate when I interfere on the detection side; on the other hand my clear-up rate is good, and it is part of my job to be successful.'

The landlord came up with a tray of sandwiches, 'Ham and beef and smoked salmon.'

'Thanks, Dick. Well done. How's the wife?'

'Not too bad, all things considered. You could ask after me, triplets at my age are no joke.' He added, 'We had been thinking of calling one after you, sir, but they are all girls.' He picked the tray that had carried the drinks and departed.

'He's doing well here,' said Coffin with a straight face. 'It's a second marriage. His first wife died young. Take a sandwich.'

Phoebe helped herself to one of smoked salmon. 'Twins and triplets are much commoner than they were,' she said. 'Almost always the result of artificial insemination.' The vodka had loosened her tongue rather more than usual.

'Don't tell Dick that,' said Coffin. 'Let's start at the beginning: I call the Jackson murders the beginning. The forensics team has gone through the murder scene gathering up whatever they can find from skin fragments and hair. These are being DNA-tested.'

'The DNA test is very sensitive and accurate now,' said Paul Masters.

'Oh yes, if we had a suspect to try it on.'

'It seems as though Mrs Jackson knew her killer. She let him in, walked into the house in front of him and he shot her in the back . . . the two girls must have heard the noise and come to see. They were then shot.' He added, 'So the motive, whatever it is, rests with Mrs Jackson. But it's guesswork, guesswork. Her son might have known something, almost certainly did, and that's why he was shot too.' Gloomily, Coffin ended, 'About the only thing that emerges to my mind is that the killer is local. Because it looks as though Dr Murray must have known or guessed something, because she was killed next.'

'I agree,' said Phoebe. 'He has to be local . . . Or she, we can't rule out a woman doing it. No physical strength needed to pull a trigger against someone who doesn't suspect you.'

'What Dr Murray knew must have been connected with those infant heads, and somehow with the Neanderthal heads found in a pit in the car park. She was very interested in them.'

'Look for a Neanderthal survivor,' joked Phoebe. She was playing her part in the investigation of Dr Murray's death and wanted to get on with it alone.

Coffin was silent. He had had an idea about the murder of Dr Murray while studying the file on her, but then he had fallen asleep.

The idea, fleeting, forgotten, sleep-drowned, was still there though.

'It's a bloody nuisance about Larry Lavender's little revolt. It gets in the way of the real work. So I expect you want to know what I am going to do about it? Keep it out of the papers and the TV news if we can . . . May not be able to, because he is bound to want publicity.'

'Call him in,' said Phoebe decisively. 'And blow his head off.' She passed over the fact that the Chief Commander's active role in the investigation of the murder of Dr Murray was not entirely to her interest.

Coffin said kindly, 'I'm going to order some coffee for you, Phoebe.' He held up his hand to the landlord. 'No, I shall wait for him to come to me.'

The landlord, who seemed well prepared (or just a good guesser), came across, 'Coffee, sir? I'll serve you that in the coffee room. Haven't pubs changed, sir, since you and I pounded the pavements in Evelyn Street.' He lowered his voice, 'I've got a chap at the bar who thinks he knows something that might help you with the killing in the University Hospital.'

Coffin got up and walked across to the bar.

'It's the fellow on the right in the blue jeans and shirt,' said the landlord. 'He works in the hospital, he's a nurse.

This is his regular pub when not working. He seems a decent sort.'

'What's his name?'

'I call him Teddy.'

Teddy drained his glass as Coffin came up to him. He had a round, jolly face, but he started up nervously, saying that he had just wondered if he could help. Of course, he recognized the Chief Commander. Miss Astley too, he added surprisingly.

He looked round the room as if he didn't want to be noticed. It was full, but no one was taking any notice of Teddy.

'These killings we're having . . . all one man, I've heard, sir.'

'It is possible.'

'It's the blood. I heard that there were two sorts where Dr Murray was found shot, hers and anothers . . . that one was HIV-infected.'

Coffin nodded. 'Well?'

'We had a patient in that day, a real bleeder, and HIV on him too . . . I just wondered. I mean, he got better and went home but . . .'

'Who was he?'

Teddy fidgeted and was silent.

Under pressure, muttering that this was all confidential and he hoped his name could be kept out of it, 'Not supposed to talk about patients, sir.' He said that the man's name was Adam Dodd, and it was all in the records.

'Have you told anyone else this?'

Teddy shook his head. 'Wasn't asked. There have been detectives in the hospital, of course, taking statements and so on, but they never spoke to me.'

Coffin went back to where the other two were sitting. 'We might have him,' he said quietly.

Phoebe Astley frowned at Paul Masters. She's getting the medicine now, he thought.

He did not go to the hospital himself, although he was

tempted. He got Paul Masters to send round a sharp request for information on Adam Dodd.

'If no one more senior is in the Incident Room, get James Whitley on to it.'

That will please them, thought Masters, a little tact wouldn't do any harm here, but 'Yes, sir' was all he said.

He returned in quicker time than he had expected (he had to admit that Whitley was both tough and efficient) with the address.

'Flat 12, Gabriel Luxembourg Buildings, Shadow Street. He's on the ground floor, because he can't manage stairs.' He added, 'If you don't mind me saying so, Chief Commander, if he's as ill as that then he doesn't sound like our killer.'

Coffin was non-committal. 'Let me see him first.'

'They won't like that,' Masters said, meaning the team investigating the murder of Dr Murray. But it's all muddled up, he added to himself; everyone is getting a finger in everyone else's pie.

'Their own fault,' said Coffin crisply. 'They should have got on to him earlier. What's Whitley going to do?'

'Going round to Gabriel Luxembourg Buildings.'

'Right, you go too, and I will come as well.'

'It's war,' Masters said to himself. Phoebe Astley, taking a hand in the Murray murder, would frown even harder.

Gabriel Luxembourg Buildings in Shadow Street was named after a popular singer in the Second City. He had drowned when he was singing at a party on a boat in the Thames which sank. He had been doing a drunken version of 'Rule Britannia' when the boat went down, which some said had offended the gods of the river, but since Gabriel, drunk or not, had succeeded in rescuing a child and dog before going under himself he was a sainted figure in the Second City.

The block of flats was plain and unpretentious, with red brick, square windows and white paint. Here and there graffiti was painted on the walls, these too in white paint, but they were of a jocular and light-hearted kind.

Paul Masters came with Coffin to find that James Whitley had already arrived. Masters looked around; no sign of CI Astley.

Then the Chief Commander's mobile rang.

'Astley here, sir. Sorry I can't be with you, urgent developments here. I will keep you informed.'

Masters looked at him in query.

'Nothing, or God knows, take your pick,' said Coffin, shortly. 'Let's get on with this.'

He pressed the doorbell. After a pause, the door opened a crack.

Adam was a very tall, thin man. He looked frail, but he was erect and he held the door firmly.

The Chief Commander introduced himself and the others.

'Takes a lot to get you to lead a raiding party.'

'Just some questions. Can we come in?'

Adam held the door open. 'Don't reckon I can stop you. Three against one.'

'We won't come in if you say no.'

'You reckon? So what it's all about? You can search the place. No drugs, no illegal whisky or baccy.'

'Thank you.' The whole party was inside. The place was clean and tidy, modestly furnished with soft pastel colours on walls and curtains.

'Want to seach the place? Go ahead. I don't know what this is about, but don't let me stop you.'

No chance of that if I order a search, said Coffin's expression at once humane, understanding and strict, but what he said was, 'Were you in the university hospital recently?'

Adam's pale blue eyes met Coffin's dark blue with an assessing gaze. He was slow to answer. Eventually, he said, 'I can see what you are getting at. I read the newspapers.'

But Coffin had read comprehension in those pale blue eyes already.

'Yes, I was there. I tripped and fell on my face. My nose took the impact. It began to bleed. Noses do bleed readily.'

Coffin nodded. There was a shadow of a bruise still on the bridge of the nose.

'And since I am a bleeder, my nose gushed blood. I value my blood, I didn't want it wasted, so I went to the hospital: I had a little op, emergency, they know me there. They plugged my nose.' He gave Coffin a half-smile. 'And then I came home, here, where I stayed quietly for the rest of the day, seeing no one, and the rest of the week.'

'No one?'

'No one. The doctor said to keep quiet, and I have to admit I didn't feel too good and I was glad to oblige. In fact, I reckon you are the only people I have seen.'

'Right,' said Coffin. 'Well, just a few more questions to clear things up. But that would be better in a more official place.' He smiled to help the thought go down. 'And there might be one or two tests to help forensics. Always best to get things over with, isn't it?'

Adam gave a smile back.

'Mind if I sit down?'

'Do, I'd be glad to myself . . . Like a drink?'

'Tea or coffee would do nicely,' said Coffin, giving a small nod to the other two, which meant: Take a look around now.

'And Adam put on his professional "I am innocent" look,' said Coffin as they left. 'You found nothing? I got nothing out of my questions – polite but evasive.'

Masters shook his head. 'Nothing.'

'Not a thing,' said Whitley. 'He's very frail . . . I don't think he's got the strength to be our killer.'

'You don't need strength.' Coffin was looking back at the windows. He could see a face staring out, and once again a memory stirred and then slid back into the darkness before he could lay a hand on it. 'Just anger and determination and a gun, and I reckon he's got the anger and he may have the gun. Anyway, I guess he is stronger than he looks.' He turned to Whitley. 'What's in his bio? What was he before he collapsed into illness?'

'An actor,' said Whitley reluctantly.

Coffin knew about actors. 'Clear it with your CI, then check whether Adam Dodd is his real name or his acting name, and find out what he's done under that or any other names. Then come to me.'

13

*Coffin says he doesn't know the time or
what day of the week it is.*

Joseph Bottom liked to think he was the one that mattered.
I care, he used to say, the others just do a job and get paid.

'If you gotta talk, you gotta talk,' he said. 'You have
to tell.'

He looked at CI Phoebe Astley with large-eyed wonder as
if she had three heads.

'I'm glad you came to me.' He hadn't, of course; he'd just
come wandering round looking for a Father Confessor and
fallen into the arms of a Mother Confessor.

'We get a lot of talk in the hospital. We pass things round.'
He moved his hands in a circle as if to show her what he
meant. 'Not supposed to talk about patients.'

'But you do?'

'This wasn't quite talking . . . Dr Murray's dead, murdered,
poor soul, and there was this talk about the blood being not
all her own.'

'So?' Phoebe didn't want to deny or acknowledge the truth
of this statement.

'A chap came in with a bad nosebleed . . . spurting all out
and around. I cleared up what I saw where he'd been sitting
in the A and E waiting room. And sometimes if it looks
necessary the blood is bottled with a little liquid. He was
one, had been in often. Then the nurse comes out and hands
me the bottle and I take it to the lab to keep it . . . I was going

175

to do this when an emergency blew up . . . woman having a fit. I was called to that and left the bottle by the wall.'

He lowered his head to look at Phoebe in apology.

She obliged him with the right answer. 'And you forgot,' she said, helping him out.

'The lady having the fit was someone I knew, does my wife's hair, and I wanted to be there if she needed a friendly face . . . She didn't, came round all neat and quick by herself. Forgotten to take her tablets, she said.'

Phoebe waited.

'When I remembered the blood and went back it was gone. Someone had taken it. At first I thought, like you would, that it had been disposed of in the right way. I asked around, keeping it tactful, but no one admitted even seeing it. Then, when we heard about Dr Murray and the two types of blood, I wondered if it was my bucket of blood.'

He stopped dead.

To get him moving again, Phoebe said, 'Thank you for telling me.'

'Then I came to thinking that Mr Dodd might have taken it himself. Some people are funny about their own blood, he's one of them. Asked the doctor once if he could have it bottled to take home . . . He wasn't let, of course. But he hung around a long time. I saw him down the corridor; he could have found it. I shouldn't have left it.'

'No,' said Phoebe. 'You shouldn't have left it.'

'I don't suppose he'd have wanted this lot, but you never know. All handled very carefully.' He studied Phoebe's face to see if she was either laughing or frowning. 'No laughing matter with him. Precautions have to be taken.'

'So when it went missing, you kept quiet and prayed? Right . . . and then you heard about the blood or bloods about Dr Murray and decided it was time to talk?'

Joe nodded.

'And you were right. Thank you.'

'I don't reckon it could have been him. He was really in pain with his nose, was still spouting when he left . . . He had it blocked up, though, but any rush would have brought the blood out fast.'

And then he realized what he had said and stopped short. 'I'm sorry, miss. I'm all muddled.'

'We all are,' said Phoebe gently. 'But you've done the right thing in talking to me.'

'And it could have spouted out as he killed Dr Murray,' said Phoebe to Coffin.

The Chief Commander looked thoughtful. He had telephoned Stella to hear what, if anything, she knew about Adam Dodd under any of his names. He had three: Adam Dodd as a TV performer, Dave Adams for the straight stage, and Archy Deacon was the name on his birth certificate. Same initials, differently arranged. Stella thought he had a fourth name for radio, but she couldn't recall that one.

She seemed to remember them all with some affection, and no, she didn't see him as a murderer, but . . .

Yes, there was always a but, thought Coffin, and he gritted his teeth to see what this but amounted to.

Stella said he had loved playing murderers; only on stage, of course. But yes, now he mentioned it, Adam was always interested in blood.

'I remember when one of our stage hands had a nosebleed and Adam was deeply troubled. Oh poor chap, he said, losing all that lovely red stuff.'

'Thanks, love,' said Coffin. 'You've been a help.'

'Oh good,' Stella sounded surprised. 'I'm always glad to be helpful.' It didn't happen very often.

'Did he show any interest in guns?'

'I don't think so. Never heard of it. But I didn't really know him well.'

'So what shall we do with Dodd?' asked Phoebe.

'Hang on to him as long as possible,' said Coffin. 'If possible until the forensic reports come in. At the moment there is no hard evidence. We don't know yet if the blood type is a match.'

'Seems likely,' said Phoebe. 'How many patients were in that day, with blood running all over them and having HIV? And Joe said he was hanging around.'

'So your picture is that Dodd comes in, nose bleeding, gets it plugged. Does he kill Dr Murray first, or after his visit to the A and E ward?'

'Oh, before. That's what starts the nosebleed?'

'But he had had an accident.'

'Well, that too; may have been what maddened him that day, pain can.'

'Well, leaving out the question of motive, why did he hang around as you put it?'

'To get his blood back.'

Coffin just looked at her.

'You do, don't you?' said Phoebe. 'If you're in a really wacky mood after killing someone, it's the sort of thing you do.'

Coffin continued looking at her. She might have been serious.

'Guns, does he have a gun? And timing, was he in the hospital at the time Dr Murray was killed? You think he killed her and his nose bled. That's your picture?' He shook his head. 'I can't quite buy it.'

'I agree that lots of points need clearing up.' Phoebe was sticking. 'Perhaps his nose hurt because he had had an accident, which is what we are told, so he came to hospital because he knew with his history he needed help, and he saw Dr Murray and killed her.'

'Why?'

'If he killed Dr Murray, then he killed the Jacksons and went out on the other shootings; he gets high on shootings. Or he hates the human race and is taking it out on them.'

The infant skulls, Coffin thought. This killer, whether Dodd or not, is not sane and not approachable. He is to be feared.

'There are quite a few incidents to be checked,' said Coffin slowly. 'If he did one, he did all of them, then some traces must turn and will link him to them.'

It was a gospel of hope, more than conviction, but you have to believe in something.

'I set up the Crime Forum so all the investigations could link up. Meld.'

All this arrangement had done so far had been to create a rebellion. So far Larry Lavender had not shown up, but when he did, all false smiles and charm, he meant to deal with him with well-honed power.

Meanwhile he had something to say to CI Astley.

'There is one thing that can be done at once; get the forensic expert analysing the blood on the floor – it's probably Diana Bloomer – and find out if there was any liquid in the blood.'

'I'll send Sergeant Abbey,' said Phoebe shortly; you did not order a Chief Inspector around in that voice, especially one who had known you in your lesser days. She began to feel a certain sympathy with Larry Lavender. 'He's been in touch with forensics.'

The answer came back with speed: Yes, there was a liquid with the blood and we could have told you before if you had asked. It is all in the report, which will shortly be on your desk.

Sadly Coffin reflected that he had irritated yet another professional. What was it a truthful aristocrat said to the unlucky Louis XVI? 'Sire, this is not a revolt, it is a revolution.'

He was beginning to feel it was his head they wanted.

Phoebe Astley, with the uncomfortable sensation that she was beginning to notice her age (no husband, no children, no lovers, she was leaving it all too late), went into the run-down little café near to Mimsie Marker's paper stall that served the best cup of coffee in the Second City.

She found herself sharing a table with Mimsie. Not too surprising, as local gossip had it that Mimsie owned the place.

'Hello.' Mimsie had long ago established friendly relations with Phoebe; you had to keep in with the police. 'How's your boss?'

'Fine,' said Phoebe cautiously.

'Hints and rumours say he's got trouble. I admire him myself, a lovely man.'

'You mustn't believe all you hear.'

'You know newspapers . . . will print anything for a good story.'

'I haven't seen anything in the press.'

'I notice you don't say there's nothing to come,' said Mimsie sharply. 'Keep your eyes on the dailies and it will . . . even *The Times*, maybe. It's New Labour, you see, give the police a whipping, and your chap might be in for one.'

'And who will do the whipping?'

'You don't know much about Larry Lavender, do you? Not his background? His ancestry . . . people don't have to be princes and dukes to have an ancestry . . . His father led the last dock strike, and his grandfather marched in 1926; there was a General Strike then. And his great-uncle was Prime Minister for a year or two. He still lives here, and Mr Coffin sorted out a mystery for him.'

Phoebe drank some coffee while she digested this. It was not good news.

'And I hear you've got Adam Dodd in durance vile.'

There was often a highly literate Mimsie peeping through her disguise, Phoebe reflected as the quotation rippled out. People often speculated where Mimsie came from. Phoebe thought she came from Babylon and had been around for millennia.

'You've heard?'

'Everyone knows. You can't keep a thing like that quiet. He's got lots of friends.'

'Has he?'

Phoebe was surprised. He hadn't struck her as the friendly type.

'Police not amongst them . . . although I believe he did have a boyfriend once who was a copper, but he had to leave. Drummed out or offered early retirement or whatever it is you do in the Force.'

Mimsie, Phoebe registered, was laughing at her.

'I don't see him as a murderer, though.'

Phoebe finished her coffee; she wanted to say, But he's all we've got.

'Vampire, yes,' said Mimsie, thoughtfully.

'I see you do know him.'

'But he'd want the blood checked, for which you can't blame him. I would myself.' Mimsie added complacently, 'But I have always been full-blooded.' Mimsie got up, saying she had left a lad in charge of the stall and who knows what a muddle he might be making.

'Mind you, by some mischance – and you can't trust a hospital to watch out for everything, and I heard he bought some blood once – he could have got the wrong blood, say of a murderer, and it got into his system and made him one.'

'It can't work like that,' said Phoebe.

'No? No, I suppose you are right.' Mimsie slung her big black bag over her shoulder, its weight registering as the shoulder went down. Not the crown jewels, thought Phoebe, but she might have a Kalashnikov in there. 'Now don't go making a Frankenstein monster out of poor Doddy, odd as he is,' she said as she departed.

'You do think he is odd then?'

'We all have our oddities, don't we, dear?' Mimsie laughed and departed. 'I'm odd myself.'

You certainly are, thought Phoebe, but shrewd with it. She realized that she had been fed some information about Adam that would bear thinking about.

What sort of a man was he?

Odd but innocent was Mimsie's worldly verdict.

Phoebe left on her own, made a few notes on the questions she would put to the doctor in the emergency ward. If he had dealt with Adam Dodd, then it was time he was questioned. She might surprise the Chief Commander by coming up with something positive.

She finished up her coffee, gathered her skirts, metaphori-cally, because she favoured a trouser suit, and departed for the hospital. In her hurry she forgot to pay for her coffee and had to turn back.

'Oh that's all right,' said the man behind the counter. 'Mrs Marker paid . . . she said you deserved it.'

Phoebe shrugged herself into her coat. Thank you, Mrs Marker, you shall be repaid. In what coin, time would show.

She walked briskly to the hospital. Why not drive? she asked herself. Because you are in an awkward mood, that's why. So she walked faster.

By a lucky chance, the same young doctor who had treated Adam Dodd was on duty that day. He had a round, cheerful face, with a confident, pleasant manner. Phoebe foresaw a bright future in medicine for him.

'Chief Inspector? Gerry Timson,' he held out his hand. 'Inspector Dover was in here earlier.'

So Harry Dover had got in first. That was typical of him, to cover the ground. A quick, brisk interview was his style.

'You don't mind if I go over the ground again?'

'No, sure. Glad to. Come into my office. I do have an office,' he grinned at her. 'Or hutch.'

It was indeed a small room, untidy with books, files and loose papers. 'A lot of us share this,' he said. There was only one chair, so they both stood.

'Yes, I know Dodd. I haven't been working here very long, but I know him, we all do in the A and E. He liked us, I think.' He smiled.

'What exactly happened that day?'

'Bearing in mind that it was the day Dr Murray was killed?' He didn't wait for an answer but turned to a large folder from which he extracted several papers clipped together. 'Not supposed to talk about patients, but this is official?'

'It is.'

'And of course, just for you.'

'Well, I will certainly be discreet . . . but it may be used.'

He grinned again. 'Okay. On your head be it. Right: he

came in early but we were busy; there had been a bus crash and also the night before two sets of football supporters had fought it out between them as well as drinking. Most of them came in with the dawn to be stitched up. I wasn't on then, but there was still a backlog when I did arrive . . . I'm only one of a team, of course, and fairly low on the pecking order.' He gave his broad smile again.

Phoebe wondered what, if anything, that smile meant, and decided it was like a full stop at the end of a sentence.

'So it was a busy day, and he had to hang around with his broken nose. Wasn't broken, more cracked, but he needed several stitches.'

'He was bleeding?'

'Sure. Freely, very freely. I believe you know about it? Well, we fixed him up, gave him a local, stitched the nose and forehead. He was still bleeding, even with his nose plugged. He wanted his blood bottled.'

'Did you do it?'

'Not me personally, but one of the nurses did her best. But liquid has to be added, else it would dry up. One of the nurses took charge, I don't know any more. I sent him out. I told him to rest. I doubt if he did.'

'Why?'

'He was excited. A few people react like that. In fact, I am told he hung around. I was too busy to keep an eye on him. A seriously wonk guy.'

Phoebe considered. 'What was he wearing when he came in?'

'You'd have to ask the nurses in reception that. By the time he got to me, he was done up in a gown ready for the op, which he enjoyed, I may say; he seemed to know the routine.'

'Where is the nurse?'

'You'll have to ask in reception. I'll help.' He put his arm round her shoulders and led her out of his office to the long reception desk.

Come on, doctor, she thought, but then it really was nice

to that feel that firm medical grip on her. And the smile too; she was getting to like that smile, as well as the faint smell of antiseptic that hung around him. Made her wonder what she smelt of.

Dr Timson addressed the whole row of faces lined up at the desk, passing over the lines of patients waiting to register.

'Which of you was here that day? Remember it?' He looked at Phoebe, who nodded. 'And took in the bleeder.' All knew the bleeder; day yes, dates?

A hand was held up, 'Adam Dodd? It was him again. It was me.' A plump girl wearing big spectacles.

'So?'

'I took his particulars, which I reckon I know by heart, sat down on a bench and . . .' A pause. 'The day of the killing. One of the killings.'

Dr Timson smiled. Got there. 'And?'

'Jenny Sledger took over . . .' She nodded. 'She's over there.'

Jenny, a nurse with a tough expression, admitted she remembered the case, which she had delivered, when the time came, to Dr Timson and his team.

'What was Dodd wearing?'

She frowned. 'Jeans, a sweater, pretty bloodstained, and a jacket. I folded them up, put them in a plastic bag, as always,' she was a brisk lady, 'and handed them over to him.'

'Was the coat heavy?'

'Light as a feather.'

No gun then. He didn't bring a gun in.

Dr Timson walked with her to the door. 'So Dodd didn't bring a gun in.'

'You read my mind.'

'Read it? I was there before you. You're not the first police officer to visit here, not by a long way, and they all look for guns. A and E departments get all the dicey woundings. Not to mention the police all over the place after the murder looking for guns and hiding places for guns. Yes, they thought of that. So don't go thinking he hid a gun here and then went to get it when he fancied a shooting.'

'You're not nearly such a nice man as I thought,' said Phoebe sadly.

'Yes, I am. Much nicer.' The grin came back. 'Give me a chance to show you. Tonight, maybe?'

Phoebe walked home, reflecting that she had a date with a doctor who was younger than she was and who might not turn up (she herself might decide not to), but that she had brought nothing good back for Coffin.

She made contact with Inspector Dover, and both came to the conclusion that Adam Dodd was not the killer. His blood had been used by another hand.

Perhaps they should suspect Dr Timson.

Coffin received the news calmly but gloomily. 'Pity. Dodd looked like a good fit. Have to eliminate him from the enquiry. I had hopes there. Going to rub Larry Lavender's face in it.'

'I'd go careful there, sir, if I were you.'

'Know something I don't, do you?'

He sounded irritable, which was not like Coffin, so this must be handled carefully.

'I'm going to see Dr Timson again. See what I can get out of him. I have an idea he knows something.'

'Get what you can.'

'Oh I will, sir.' Tonight, 8.30, at the Café Blanc. 'I'll report back.' But not everything.

She then passed on what Mimsie had told her about Larry Lavender.

To her relief, it made Coffin laugh. 'It's all in his records, but I don't hold it against him. Often felt like going on strike myself. Still, I'll bear it in mind, and thanks for reminding me. Wonder how Mimsie got to know? We ought to employ her. Oh, and watch with Dr Timson . . . He's a great womanizer.'

And he put the telephone down quickly before she could come back at him.

* * *

When Coffin let himself into St Luke's Tower, there was a sweet-scented smell on the air, which indicated the passage down the staircase of Stella. It was another new perfume, not one of the sharp spicy scents she used, but a new one. Not really new, she had said, started life in Paris in about 1890 and is now having a comeback. We can smell like ladies again, not refugees from a brothel. Coffin liked it.

The small cat was sitting on the stairs looking down at him.

'Hello cat, all on your own?'

'She is not,' Stella called down the stairs.

Ahead of her floated the sweet fragrance and behind came a more savoury smell from the kitchen.

'You're cooking, Oh good, I'm hungry.'

'Fish,' said Stella. 'Salmon. We can share it with the cat.'

'Invited any other guest to dinner?' Coffin continued up the staircase.

Stella was not wearing very much, a pale printed chiffon dress with narrow shoulder straps.

'Are you warm enough in that?' enquired Coffin. 'It's chilly in here.'

'Oh, quite warm enough, I'm trying out one of the new designer dresses. Do you like it?'

'Very much. You could go to bed in that.' It did look like a nightdress. 'You could try that later.'

'It's not exactly mine, or not altogether: it's for a new production of the Coward play later in the year, his centenary, you see.' She swung round, flirting the skirt. 'I think it has the feeling of a nineteen thirties dress while being of the twenty-first century.'

They talked quietly during the meal, of which the cat took a full cat's share, which is larger than a human's share.

Stella told Coffin about her plans for the new season and how she hoped to get Daisy Moore for a leading role in a Shaw play she meant to stage if she could get backing.

And Coffin told her that he had been unpleasant to Phoebe Astley and now regretted it.

'Sheer malice and ill humour on my part,' he said with a sigh.

'She'll get her own back.'

'I hope so, seems only fair. She's a good officer. You know about the little insurrection?'

Stella nodded. 'It'll come to nothing.'

'Spoken like a loyal wife.'

Stella considered. 'Which, on the whole, I am.'

'There might be a bit of fuss in some of the papers. I might even make the BBC news. If they want to interview, shall I say yes?' he asked lightly.

Without hesitation, Stella said, 'Yes.'

In her world there was no such thing as bad publicity. Might be different for him, Coffin thought. But after all, what did he want from life? He had a job he loved, give or take the odd patch, he had a wife he loved too, and – he looked down at something nuzzling at his leg – he had a cat who seemed to like him.

He didn't want to retire to the country and keep bees.

'Do you mind if I take my work to my workroom and get on with it alone?'

'Of course not. I've got some work to do as well. Shall I bring you some coffee?'

Coffin retired to his room, the cat coming too, the one to go to sleep on the desk and the other to sort his papers, read and think.

Reading the records then thinking was more a part of detection than the outside world understood. It wasn't all questioning suspects, checking alibis and being the hard man. That too, but in the end understanding the picture as a whole was what counted.

You needed to be a good, quick reader too, he decided as he assembled all his papers and got down to work, at intervals removing a furry tail that seemed to spread over them, flipping gently with pleasure.

'Make a copper of you yet,' he said, displacing it with care, remembering that not far from the tail were a set of sharp claws.

He worked slowly through the case notes of each murder, beginning with Mrs Jackson and her daughters, down to the attack on Marie Rudkin.

He remembered the infant skulls ranged round Dr Murray. He saw again the Neanderthal heads in the pit, with the one alien head.

He picked out from his collection of paper the photograph of the body of Dr Murray on the museum floor, circled by the skulls and in a pool of blood. He had requested an enlarged copy of this photograph.

There was the face looking through the window, just as he remembered it. Enlargement had brought the face forward and bigger, but it was fuzzy, lacking definition.

The face of a killer? Or the face of an innocent if curious bystander? At the moment an unanswerable question.

But there were some things he could say about the face: first it was plumpish, second it was the face of a man, third it was not an old face, and finally it was the face of someone who knew his way around the hospital.

Mustn't stretch it too far; of course, if he was the killer, then he certainly knew what had taken place in the museum, but he might just be an interested passer-by.

Must have a look at the passage behind that way. If it was a passage. The photograph did not make it clear.

Coffin put the photograph down, retaining the feeling that somewhere he had seen that face before. He knew that face.

The little cat moved forward to stare in his face, not purring, but interested.

He sat thinking and gently stroking the cat. Then Coffin stood up and went to the window: there is something in common with each victim.

He picked up the phone and rang Paul Masters.

'Paul, I know it's late. This is what I want you to do

tomorrow morning. Early. I want the details of Mrs Jackson's last two working years. Likewise Mrs Pomeroy. And Mrs Rudkin. All the records should be there. Also check who were the midwives or nurses in charge of Lia Boston's childbirths. That will do for the moment.'

Oh good, thought Paul Masters. Only about six months' work in one morning. He came back, 'Oh sir, there was a call from Inspector Lavender earlier . . . he'd like to see you.'

'Right,' said Coffin briskly. He thought about it: soon, but not too soon. 'Tomorrow, late morning.'

Stella came in just then with the coffee. 'Hope you weren't waiting for this; I got caught up in some work of my own.'

She was no longer wearing the chiffon dress but trousers and a silk shirt. Coffin thought she looked just as good if not better. How is it that men wear the same clothes all the day whereas a woman can change from one style to another? Why aren't we like that?

Then he thought of himself in a floating chiffon dress and had to laugh. I haven't got the legs for it.

'What are you laughing at?'

'At myself.'

Stella had brought with her two cups and a small silver coffee pot from which she poured some throbbingly strong coffee. He had known her say modestly that it had been her great-grandmother's and had come down to her, but Coffin knew that she had bought it off a stall in Greenwich Market. When taxed with this, Stella had said that it might have been her great-grandmother; it was certainly someone's great-grandmother, so why not hers? It was what she called a publicity lie: only offered to certain people at certain times.

'You don't look as worried as you did.'

'I ought to; my friend Larry Lavender wants to see me tomorrow.'

'Mimsie Marker is on your side.'

'It's not a war.' It might be a fight, but he could deal with Lavender, might even enjoy it. He liked the man, a good copper when he didn't get political.

'It will be if Mimsie gets going. Good for the sale of papers.'

'I'll have to have a word with her.'

'Hard to control Mimsie.'

'Wouldn't dream of trying. But she's a worldly lady. I think I can get her to see how to play it.'

Stella was fiddling with a small silver spoon. 'I went to see Margaret Murray's husband today. He did my hair once or twice, still does when I feel I can afford his prices.'

'How are they?'

'How you might expect. What people always say when interviewed by the TV or radio: shattered. Turned inside out, not knowing where to go or what to do. Natasha seemed under the worse strain, though. She didn't want to talk to me, but she did a bit and I think I helped. I hope so. Such a clever girl, easy to like. Her husband's rather a honey. I could see that he minded for Nat.'

'All there, were they?'

'Yes, I think they are living together for the moment, till they sort themselves out.' It was going to take time. She was still twisting the spoon round and round.

'No guilt there, though?'

'No guilt.' She had to have the spoon twisted into two soon.

Coffin looked at her lovingly. 'I ought to send you round all the victims' families and see what you come back with.'

Almost nervously, she asked, 'Have you been to see Marie Rudkin?'

'I thought you had.'

'So I have.' She put down the spoon. 'I didn't tell you, but when I talked to Marie Rudkin she said she thought she would soon remember the face of the man with the gun.' Stella added, 'She was serious. Ill, but she knew what she was telling me.'

Coffin listened quietly to what Stella had to say. Soberly and with conviction, he said, 'Tell her not to repeat that to anyone else. Not a word.'

14

Almost the last day.

The morning was bright, clear and cold. A telephone call from the vet said that Gus was ready to be collected; the sooner the better was the implication that Coffin understood, because a bored Gus was a snappy Gus. Especially if they had had him on a diet, as seemed likely.

He settled with Stella that he would collect the dog while she would shop for some of his favoured food while working out how to arrange the meeting between Gus and the cat. Gus had been on friendly terms with their old cat, an animal of dignity and power, not easily crossed, but this new one was small and frisky.

As promised, he collected Gus, who met him with enthusiasm tempered with reproach. His illness and the subsequent operation must clearly have been Coffin's fault. Still, Gus conveyed, it was nice to see him again and he would be forgiven in time. He conveyed nothing about Stella, because in the intervening weeks he had forgotten her, that being the way his memory worked, but once he saw her again, he would recall everything and all affection would come rushing back.

He led Gus back up in the lift, through his outer office where Paul Masters held sway, assisted by the couple of secretaries. Masters greeted Gus with pleasure, getting in return a measured careful look together with a slight wag of the tail, but when Masters followed them in with a bowl of water and biscuit bones, he got a more enthusiastic reception.

Masters retreated. Gus took up his usual spot under the Chief Commander's desk, where Coffin settled himself for the morning's work.

'Oh Paul, when's Lavender coming in?'

'About midday . . . I thought that would suit you? I can ring back and change it.'

'No, let him come.'

On the desk in front of Coffin, Masters had arranged a neat pile of newspapers, the locals to one side, the London broadsheets in the middle, and the popular scandal and picture papers to the right.

Coffin figured in all of them. He read each story carefully: ATTACK ON POLICE CHIEF, CRITICAL ATTACK ON DISTINGUISHED CHIEF COMMANDER, down to WATCH IT COPPER.

The burden of each story, however, was supportive of him, jokes apart. He had to accept that he made a good butt for jokes, but there was more praise than mockery.

'I might have got a peerage out of this if the House of Lords wasn't being abolished,' he said to Masters.

'You might get one of those working peerages, sir.'

'Yes, I doubt I'd get away without work coming in.' Coffin pushed the papers aside. 'Wonder what Lavender made of his press.'

'He wasn't named.'

'Better get down to work before Lavender arrives . . .' Coffin looked at Masters. 'Something's up, I can see it in your face.'

'Lia Boston's husband wants to see you.'

'Not sure I want that. It's going to drive Larry Lavender even further up the wall of protest. Isn't he leading the team into the Bostons' killings?'

'Boston insists on seeing you.'

'He's not exactly my favourite criminal, and I think he knows that. He's a devious bugger.'

'He trusts you. He thinks you are honest.'

'So is Lavender.'

'He admits that, but he thinks in certain circumstances Lavender might stitch him up. You wouldn't.'

'Well, thank him for that vote of confidence. Not quite sure what to make of it coming from him. And he's in those "circumstances", is he? Come on now, you know what he's talking about.'

'No, sir. But knowing Boston, I can guess: something illegal that he's guilty of.'

'Which covers a wide range.'

'He says that the whole of CID and the uniformed lot have marked his card.' He hadn't put it as politely as that. They certainly had his name marked in red, an honour well earned over the years.

'Where is he now?'

'Downstairs, upright. PC Diver on the front desk wouldn't give him a seat.'

'First time he's been upright in years.'

'He made that joke himself, sir.'

'You went down to see him,' accused Coffin.

'Yes, he's always good for a laugh, and I speak as one who has helped put him away more than once. Anyway, I really went down to see he was stowed away somewhere where he won't meet Larry Lavender and give him an interview for the press.'

'Show him in now, then. Let's get it over before Lavender bowls in. And be here yourself, and take notes. I want a witness.'

He sat watching as Tom Boston came in, prepared, as Coffin could see, to be aggressive. Good, Coffin thought, aggression I can handle. He was a short man, with a crest of thick hair, always beautifully dressed. Had his suits made in Milan, so fable had it. Not London tailoring anyway, Coffin reckoned, jacket lapels too curving and swoony, jacket itself too loose, and trousers beautiful and dancing free. Nothing Jermyn Street about them.

He waited. Let Boston speak first. Then he remembered that the chap had lost his wife and children in a terrible killing.

'I'm sorry about Lia and the children.'

'That's what all you lot say first off. Said it when they took me into identify Lia and the kids, but then they changed back as if they thought I'd done it.'

'You're not under any suspicion, Tom.'

'I bet they wish they could pin it on me.'

'Is that why you wanted to see me? Why did you?'

Tom Boston leant across the desk. 'Sympathy minute over, is it? No, I came because I had something to say to you. One of Lia's friends told me that Lia said I knew something about this serial gunman. Perhaps that's why Lia was killed, she said, looking at me as if it was my fault. What I want to say is that I don't know anything, never did and never said anything to Lia. She was making it up, like she did sometimes.'

'She must have had something to go on,' said Coffin.

'That group of friends of hers . . . I never liked them.' He shook his head. 'Got it from them.'

Coffin studied Boston's face, probably not lying, but he was a professional, you couldn't tell. He was on the fidget though.

'You didn't come just to tell me that.'

Boston swallowed and began to mutter something.

'Speak up.'

It was more a case of spit it out. As well as Lia, Tom had a wife across the Channel, in Germany. He had married Sophy first, so the marriage to Lea was bigamous. Tom could see that this was illegal, but he was inclined to sniff at it. 'Don't know why we married, we could have lived together, everyone does, and then no bother. But now . . .' He shrugged his shoulders; one was slightly out of kilter with the other, Coffin noticed, which perhaps explained the expensive tailoring.

'It gave you a motive for killing Lia,' filled in Coffin.

'Only to you lot. Not to anyone in the real world.' He had tears in his eyes. 'And you know what? I had to identify my wife and children. Well, I knew them all right, blood and torn-apart faces and all.'

'Before you go, can you give me the names of the friends of your wife?'

Tom looked vague. 'One is called Letty, and another Sheila, I don't know more.' He pursed his lips. 'She talked about the Walkers . . . had a capital letter, the word did, I could feel it. She was good with words, my Lia.' The tears ran down his nose.

'What did you make of that?' Coffin asked Paul Masters when Tom Boston had taken himself off.

Coffin was silent for a moment. Then: 'Those women must be interviewed.'

'Done so already, sir.'

'Again. They may be important.'

They could be at the heart of something. He knew not what, but it had death in it.

The Walkers, he thought. Well, let's have a go, let's try walking with them.

Larry Lavender arrived in time, early in fact, because he wanted to have a few probing words with Paul Masters on the state of the Chief Commander's morale. Not that he expected to get much out of Masters, whom he classed as a high-grade Chief Commander supporter, but he had known Masters a long while. They had worked together once and he had long fancied Masters's wife, who had proved to be one of those who make beckoning noises but are untakeable. He had suspected Masters of having put her up to it.

With all this behind him, he thought he would be able to read Masters.

'How's the CC?' this being how he spoke of Coffin, although not how he thought of him. A hiatus there. He liked him, admired him even, but sometimes felt he could kill him. Someone would kill Coffin one day, he was convinced, and it might be his wife. Now Stella Pinero . . . she was something else again. Lavender would not want her dead. He wanted her to die of old age. Something that his own wife – they were apart now, and might remain that way as far as he was concerned – had cattily remarked was approaching fast. Horrible woman, his wife, not the adorable Stella, and he could not now remember why he had married her, except for feeling it had to do with male lust.

'The Chief Commander's in a good mood,' said Masters, which was more or less true.

'Be the better for seeing me.'

'Of course, Larry.'

'Knock and go in?'

'Just go in. He is expecting you. No need to knock, he's very democratic.' Masters smiled.

Lavender smiled back, straightened his back and marched in. 'Hello, sir.'

'No need for sir,' said Coffin, standing up. 'We've worked together in the past.'

'Thanks for seeing me.'

He's nervous, thought Coffin. Never thought I'd see Larry Lavender nervous.

'Thought I ought to come and talk things over.' He waited for the Chief Commander to speak, but since he did not, Lavender went on, 'Explain what happened and why.'

'I think I know.'

'I don't think you do, sir.' He was determined to get that 'sir' in again. 'I'm good at what I do, I think you'd give me that, sir, I get results. But do they get noticed? Yes, in the records and in the convictions, but the big crimes, the ones that get in the papers . . . the big murders: the Rugely murder, the Fraser Dean kidnapping, the Service strangler, my great-uncle's case . . . they are yours, or they get your name on them. Yes, right, you were the one, sir, who saw through any deceit or camouflage to the right killer, but I was on the team of at least one of those cases, and we would have got there . . .'

He's definitely nervous, Coffin summed up. Why?

Then an illumination lit up his mind: he knows something I

don't, and it's for me. In my favour. Very much in my favour, or he wouldn't be so edgy.

Not the newspapers, they'd had their say. TV, that's it. What was that programme called? *This Week in the World.* Always got good ratings.

'Did you pick up anything about a group called the Walkers?' he asked.

'Don't think so. Why?'

'Just wondered. I heard them mentioned.'

Larry Lavender shook his head. 'That's your style, sir, you pick up something and run with it.'

'Is that how it looks?'

'You were like a cancer, sir, growing inside us.'

Real, bitter feeling there. Coffin took in his face. 'Are you all right, Larry?' he said gently. 'No, I can see you're not.'

He went to the drawer in his desk and pulled out a bottle of whisky.

'Come on, have some of this.'

'I'm not allowed,' groaned Lavender.

Stella, too, came across the Walkers. The name came up in one of her meetings with Letty and Sheila. The word just came in to their conversation. Not exactly a club, nor an institution, more of an occasion. Not like the Royal Garden Party, more like all getting on the right train together.

There was certainly a feeling of movement there. After all, the Walkers presumably walked.

Stella walked herself; she did not have to walk to work because her theatre and her home were part of the same Victorian complex of buildings, but sometimes she crossed the road to the ancient churchyard, older by far than the church, and now a peaceful small park. You walked over the dead, and Stella for one knew it, although not everyone did, but the grass was thick over their bones and to her it never seemed sacrilege. Sometimes she took Gus, but he was never allowed to pollute the grass; for that purpose she led him down the road to a large patch of rough ground by the old canal. And she took a little trowel and plastic bag. In the old churchyard Gus had been known to look longingly at one of the monuments that survived but he had been trained to do no more than look, tempting as they must seem to him and his back leg. She had already done the shopping for him, as required, and when she got home this evening there Gus would be. It was to be hoped he would like the cat. Tolerate, maybe; perhaps like was expecting too much.

She took a deep, happy breath. At times, as this morning, she walked round it. The Second City was not overly full of grassy open spaces. Especially one that was almost your own space with no one else there.

But today there was someone, a young woman sitting on the bench by the tree. She had a lovely face, half hidden by dark spectacles. There was a bruise down one side of her face.

'Natty? It is Natasha, isn't it?'

The girl looked up. 'Yes, thank you.' Her voice was low and hoarse. 'Miss Pinero.'

'Are you all right? Can I do anything.'

'No, thank you. I'm fine.'

She certainly didn't look it.

'That's a nasty bruise on your cheek.'

Natasha touched her cheek with a forefinger. 'I banged into something.'

So you did, thought Stella, what was it? A tree or a fist? Gently, she said, 'I don't think it's a good idea to sit out here in the cold.' There was a damp wind too.

'I was just having a rest . . . I've been for a walk.' Natasha stood up, straightening her back in way that made it clear she didn't want sympathy. It was obvious that she was not going to respond to Stella's implied questions on the lines of: What's up? And who hit your face?

'Right. Well, take care. It's really cold today.' Her coat and dress looked too thin for the day.

Indifferently, Natasha said, 'I didn't notice. It's peaceful here in the park. And they're all dead, aren't they?'

'Long dead,' agreed Stella.

Stella hesitated. It was not her business to act as Sister Samaritan to anyone, least of all to a girl who was pushing her away. Besides, she had a bundle of work waiting for her in the theatres. So she walked on to get into her own world again, not this chilly, achingly strange one in which Natasha seemed stuck.

But her kind heart, which for professional reasons she kept hidden, made her turn round.

Natasha was still standing where she had left her. Stella took one pace towards her.

'Have you ever seen the theatre backstage?'

Natasha shook her head silently.

'Come with me now. I'll give you a look round, and we can have a cup of coffee. No need to worry – I've trained them to make a decent cup.'

Natasha stood looking at Stella. Suddenly, she said, 'Yes, please.' Like a schoolgirl offered a treat.

She looked like a schoolgirl too, so thin and young. On impulse Stella put an arm round the thin shoulders and gave a friendly hug. As she did so she felt a shiver run through Nat's body.

Stella let her arm drop away, and said nothing more until they were in her office with the coffee ordered. It was a small room, crowded with all the impedimenta of an active theatrical life: programmes, scripts, books and photographs, many photographs.

The coffee came, hot and strong, as Stella had promised. Why was she taking this trouble with the girl? Not her usual way of managing things at all. Cool detachment at work, with all sensility and emotion reserved for home.

But this girl worried her.

'It was all the heads,' she said suddenly. 'It's all been wrong since the Neanderthal heads were found in the pit. Babies' heads.'

'You saw them?'

'No, but cousin Margaret did. And she saw one head was not so old. That worried her, I think.'

'Why would it do that?'

Natasha shrugged. 'Don't know . . . But she was clever. Sensitive, picked things up.' She raised up her cup and began to drink the coffee. 'I think she was checking if that other skull had come from the museum.'

'And had it?'

'I don't know. You must ask your husband that. It was the babies' skulls that she didn't like. Don't blame her, poor little souls. Babies can have a thin time if they aren't lucky.'

'Yes, I know that,' said Stella. She remembered the child of one of the singers in a musical she had starred in; the kid used to come to rehearsals and performances in a box turned into a cradle. That child usually looked well fed and loved, but she knew of others that were not, while at times even that infant had a pinched, anxious look out of order with its age. Some animals had that look too.

'If she hadn't gone looking in that museum, she wouldn't have been killed.'

'You think so?'

'She was seen by the wrong person. Or maybe she said something that alerted that person.'

'Could have been something like that . . . but these killings seem arbitrary, as if the killer just went after anyone.'

'Oh no, there's always children involved.'

Stella was silenced.

'Hadn't you noticed? And then she was laid out with all those children's skulls around her.'

'Did you see her?' Stella was surprised.

'No, but I've been around the hospital enough to know one or two people.'

'Yes, I know one or two, just casual friends.'

'Oh, friends . . . who knows who's a friend? Friends can be just as murderous as enemies, if they feel like that. I dare say Margaret thought he was a friend . . . always so helpful, lifting and carrying, opening the doors, keeping order . . . till he killed her.'

Stella looked at her quietly. 'Who are you talking about?' A picture came into her mind. A figure politely opening doors, moving trolleys, mopping floors. 'Are you talking about Joe? Are you calling him the killer?'

'Oh, Joe, poor Joe, how did he get dragged in?' She shook her head. 'I may not be the killer, but I am the murderer. There, I am confessing.'

'She said she was confessing, that she was the murderer.' Stella stroked the cat who was on her lap while keeping an eye on Gus who was watching her and the cat.

'That's very unlikely,' said Coffin.

Hesitantly, Stella said, 'I think she was accusing Joe.'

'He was checked over for the murder of Dr Murray and cleared.'

'And you think it is one man for all the killings?'

'Not just me,' observed Coffin mildly. 'The judgement of the whole Crime Forum.'

Stella put the cat on Coffin's knee. 'You have a go. I'll soften up Gus.'

Coffin checked Gus with keen, policemanly eye. 'He looks calm enough.'

'I wouldn't like to leave them alone together.' She patted Gus. 'I think you ought to see Natasha. Interview her.'

'Why me? Phoebe Astley could do it. Another woman. If it's really necessary at all.'

'I think she'd trust you.'

Coffin said slowly, 'She might be unwise to trust a copper. Yes, I'll see her, but she'll have to wait her turn, I'm busy tomorrow.' He smiled at his wife. 'It'll be your turn to take Gus for his morning walk.'

'Isn't it always?'

The next morning was misty and chill. Gus showed only a moderate enthusiasm for his morning exercise (recommended by the vet, no friend of Gus who had given his leg a nip), but he consented to be dragged forward on his leash. He became more interested as he realized that several new scents had been added to various trees and lamp-posts during his absence. One smell in particular was promising: near ovulation it said, and soon ready to mate. He must keep a look-out.

'All right, Gus,' said Stella, pulling on the lead. 'We all know you are keen to perpetuate your genes, but not here and not with that lamp-post.'

They moved on, with Gus now taking the lead. He had remembered a walk from the past. He began to smell water. He liked a swim. It was an occasion of innocent pleasure causing your mistress the utmost alarm and disorder, since there is nothing more difficult to handle than a wet dog.

Stella did not resist; he was on the leash, and even Gus could not get in for a swim when tethered. A visit to the canal was a quick and easy walk, so she could soon be home and back at work. She too liked the canal. There was a certain romance to it; neglected and unused now, it belonged to the Second City's industrial past.

The mist began to lift as they came along the canal, which curved out of sight in the distance. Two people were standing on the bank, just on the curve. To her surprise, she recognized Natasha. She was wearing trousers and a long dark coat, while her companion was a man, more lightly dressed. They seemed to be arguing, and he had his hand on Natasha's arm.

Then, to Stella's alarm, she saw Natasha jump into the canal, followed at once by the man. She recognized Natty's husband, Jason. Grabbing her mobile phone she dialled 999 and shouted, 'Man in the canal,' as she ran.

The man's head appeared on the surface, then disappeared again. Natasha did not show.

Stella wrenched off her shoes, disentangled herself from Gus, then jumped into the water, striking out towards the spot where they had gone down with the thought: I wish I was a stronger swimmer.

She heard a splash as Gus came too.

Ahead of her she saw the man's head surface. He was struggling, no swimmer he, to remain afloat, but something was pulling him down.

'Natasha,' she gasped. 'Hang on, I'll do what I can.' Peering through the water, she thought she could see the girl, but even as she looked she slid away, dragging the man with her.

But so it would have been if Gus had not got hold of the man's collar. No lifesaver, just a dog grabbing something that floated. An extra large fish, maybe.

Stella came level with the man just as Gus was considering dropping this awkward catch; he changed his mind, puzzled but willing, as his mistress said, 'Stay, Stay,' loudly while getting her arms round his catch.

Stella could hear the police arriving, in the distance but getting closer. She had just enough mirth and breath left in her to wonder what the police would make of their Chief's wife in the water with dog and man.

She had no idea how she looked with hair streaming, weeds on her face and mascara spreading round her eyes.

'There's a girl still in there,' Stella managed to get out as, struggling and choking, the three of them – dog, Natty and Jason – were dragged out of the water by the police.

'Did she jump or was she pushed?'

Stella managed to put the question at last to the Chief Commander as he drove her home from the hospital where she and Gus had had to stay until passed fit and well.

'They separated us,' said Stella with some indignation.

'Dogs aren't allowed in hospitals, you know that,' said Coffin patiently. 'Even heroic rescue dogs.'

Gus had spent an hour in the nurses' sitting room, before a fire, having been praised, dried and given some biscuits. He was glad to be praised since he had often known grumbles when he returned from total immersions, dripping and smelling. He smelt now.

Coffin glanced down at him. 'He could do with a bath.'

'Do I smell as bad as him?'

'Pretty near. That canal could do with cleaning.' He looked at Stella assessingly.

'They did give me a few injections in there, against everything from cholera to the plague to white dog disease as far as I could make out,' admitted Stella, answering his unspoken question.

'What's white dog disease?'

'I don't know. I just made that up. I thought it might make you laugh.'

'No, I'm not laughing.' He knew how close she had come to losing her own life. 'I love you, Stella.'

'You can't stand by and watch someone drown.'

'No. You can't. And that's why I love you. But once is enough. Promise me. A quiet life from now on.'

Stella reached out to touch his wrist. 'A fairly quiet life, I promise.'

Coffin took his eyes off the road for just a second to give one of those fond, half-smiling looks that she loved.

CI Astley came in from the outer room where she had been talking with Paul Masters.

'Sorry to interrupt, sir, but I should have told you' – never use the word 'forgot' had been one of the earliest bits of training – 'that forensics found a letter inside an inner pocket of Natasha's jacket.'

'A suicide note?'

'Looks like it, sir. But unluckily the blue ink has run so badly that it is impossible to read, but forensics are hoping to bring it up.'

Coffin digested the information. Then he said, 'Have you seen Larry Lavender lately?'

He didn't know what answer he expected, but he got nothing. Phoebe just shook her head. She had known for a long while that silence is a good answer to some questions.

Aren't we all wondering? she said to herself. 'Oh, there's one thing, sir. I had a quick look at the letter myself to see what I could make of it. Nothing, except for one large letter W, written so firm and hard it tore into the paper.'

It was impossible to work out the word, but Phoebe thought it might be Wergild: Anglo-Saxon body price. But maybe she was being imaginative.

15

Will Christmas ever come?

Death is a chancer, unexpectedly slipping under the fence to join the party without a ticket. All the murder victims had been taken by surprise. Natasha, who claimed to be the killer, had opened the door to death.

But one victim, Marie Rudkin, was pushing death back. And Larry Lavender was conducting his own fight.

'There is something I should have told you.' Stella's voice was urgent. 'Today, in the hospital, while I was waiting to be set free . . . it felt like that . . . I heard one of the nurses say to another that Mrs Rudkin was sitting up and taking food and talking.'

'Glad to hear it.' Then, delicately, because he did not want to upset Stella on this day of all days, 'Did you get to tell her not to talk about knowing who attacked her?'

'I haven't seen her alert again yet. She was unconscious, on a life-support machine, when I called back. I haven't been since.' Didn't really have a chance this morning . . .

I was waiting, Stella said to herself, till she was conscious. And now she is.

Stella looked at Gus sleeping by the fire with the little cat lying across him. 'I'm going to the hospital myself, Gus, so you keep the home fires burning. And don't answer the telephone.'

Gus rolled a lazy eye at her. As if I would, it said.

Stella made her way to where her car stood. She was very

tired and her limbs felt heavy, but she knew there was a strength inside her that would not let her down. She would drive to the hospital; she would see Marie Rudkin, and if Marie wanted to talk and felt able to do so she could talk to Stella.

That way lay safety. What two people knew was safer than only one. There was a fallacy in there somewhere, but she clung to the thought.

As Stella set out for the hospital, Larry Lavender was sitting waiting for the consultant to see him. In the ordinary way, Larry would have been glad because she was a lovely-looking lady, just the sort he fancied, but he was discovering that there was nothing like anxiety to lower the libido.

This was the day when she would deliver the results of the last test. He dreaded it. He felt she would be giving him a judgement of death approaching. Oh, she'd wrap it up, suggest treatments, palliatives, to hold things up. What was the phrase: Remission? He was aware that this worked for some people, but he just knew it wouldn't for him. He was about to be doomed.

So he sat there on the bench and waited for Dr Lemming to arrive. 'Come on, lady,' he muttered. 'Let the axe fall, I promise not to scream.'

Still no consultant. He felt like standing up and crying, I am going home, I am cured, I am better.

Indeed, he felt in much less pain. He wasn't sure if this gave him hope or not.

Then his beautiful consultant appeared round the corner, carrying several folders under her arm, and beckoned him to follow her.

In one of those folders, he concluded, was his life and death.

He went in, she closed the door behind him, and smiled, 'Now, Mr Lavender.'

Some twenty minutes or so later, Larry Lavender came out of the room, closing the door quietly behind him.

Then he took a deep breath. He felt he could do with a double whisky, no, a triple whisky, but being in the hospital he would have to make do with with coffee.

He swung right in the direction of the coffee-shop. As he did so he saw Stella Pinero come through the entrance. Ah, there was a woman, he reminded people. He watched her gossiping with people, then he avoided eye contact.

Stella hurried into the ward. Marie Rudkin was in a small room to the left of the swing doors, lying propped up against pillows. She smiled at Stella. 'Hello.' Her husband was sitting by her bed, holding her hand. 'So here I am, back in the world.' Her voice was weak, but clear.

'I am glad, I really am glad. How do you feel?'

Marie frowned. 'I couldn't go to a party or give one. But yes, I feel so much better. I can remember . . .'

She stopped.

Paul gripped her hand tighter, so tight that she withdrew it with a smile and shake of the head.

'Don't push yourself,' he said. He looked at Stella. 'I told her she shouldn't do that.'

Stella nodded. 'Quite right.'

'I think I must talk, I am beginning to remember things.' She smiled at Stella, 'And then there are things I did not know . . . they discovered while I was unconscious that I'm pregnant.'

'Oh Marie, I am pleased.'

'Yes, and all seems well . . . not miscarrying or anything.'

'And you're not going to,' said her husband.

'Three months gone,' said Marie. '*And I never knew*. You've got to admit, that's something to come round to.'

The door opened and in came Coffin. He looked surprised when he saw Stella, but he didn't speak to her. 'I had a message that you wanted to talk to me.'

'Yes, I wanted to tell you that I remember the face of the man who shot me.'

'Oh Marie, dear,' said Paul. 'I wish you wouldn't go on.'

'There isn't any more to go on about,' said Marie. 'That's all I have to say. I can describe him . . . a bit, anyway.' She leant back on her pillows and closed her eyes.

'Tell me,' Coffin began.

'Tell you anything,' said Marie, her eyes still closed. 'A dark face, very dark, plump . . .'

She's describing Joe, thought Stella. 'Joe,' she whispered to her husband.

He shook his head. To Marie, he said, 'Have you told anyone?'

'May just have said I remembered,' she muttered.

'Stop questioning her,' ordered her husband.

Be glad to, thought Coffin. 'You're safe now,' he said to her quietly. 'I may know that face.'

Behind him a door opened. Stella swung round and called out, gripping his arm.

'Yes, I know that face,' Coffin said, turning to look. 'I saw it through the window in the museum where Dr Murray lay.' He had seen it dimly, now he saw it clearly.

Marie opened her eyes. Recognition came into them because the man, dressed in hospital cleaner's overalls, held a gun.

'I will kill the lot of you,' said Sam. 'I have enough bullets, and I have done it before. One, two, three, four.'

He looked first at Marie, and then directed his gaze at Stella. 'Why, why?' she heard herself say.

Sam was willing to talk. 'If you want to know, it started with Mrs Jackson. She knew me and I knew her because she was a nurse, a baby nurse.'

'A midwife,' whispered Stella. Keep him talking, a voice inside her murmured.

'She watched me going round the museum – the one with the babies' heads.' His voice dropped to a mutter. 'She said I went there too often. "I am going to get you away from that place, it's not good for you."'

Stella thought about all those tiny skulls, and she agreed with Mrs Jackson. She wondered also about the doctor who had initially set up the museum. A man of science, or a man obsessed?

'"I am going to cure you," old Jackson said. "I am going to see you get away from that place."

'After that I didn't mind killing her . . . especially as I got paid, although the money wasn't much.'

Stella flinched as she heard what he said. Money?

'Cure me?' Sam was laughing. 'Not good for me? The cheek of her. I am the scholar of the skulls.' He repeated the words with relish. 'I know everyone, I have dusted them – no one else did – stroked them.' He waved his gun. 'I have this gun, and others and I know how to use them. Guns and skulls . . . when she said that, the two parts of me came together. If you have a gun, you are someone.' His eyes shone. 'I was a god with a gun.'

'He's mad,' thought Stella. Behind her, she heard Coffin move. Oh, be careful, she thought, he has a gun and I am in front.

But Sam was talking on. 'She said to me, "You must have been abused as a child, so I am going to help you." "No, I wasn't," I said. "I lived in a home for lost kids and it suited me. We beat each other up sometimes, but nothing to count." And you could bet our keepers did not interfere, or they might have got it. It was the lovely museum that made me a god. Joe got me work . . . remember Joe?'

Stella nodded.

'I wouldn't kill Joe, Joe's a gent. I killed Mrs J. because I was paid. It was a job, at first anyway, but I had to kill the others, because they knew me.'

'Dr Murray,' began Coffin.

Stella gave her husband a backward kick on the ankle. 'Shut up.' Be a husband, not a policeman, she wanted to say.

But Sam had heard Coffin. 'Dr Murray, now that was a real shame in a way. She was a scholar of the skulls, like I was, but she saw me stroking them. "My god, you're mad," she said. God and madness, funny how she coupled them.

So I killed her. And I sprinkled a bit of extra blood around
. . . I was a blood carrier in the hospital; some was kept for
what they called study and future use, the rest disposed of. I
gave her some second-rate stuff. Just a bit extra, to go with
her own blood . . . Well, she deserved some treatment: she
recognized the skull I buried . . . the one with blood dried on
it. And then she saw the gold ring . . . that was off a stiff in
the mortuary . . . I stole it. I did steal a bit, we all did, this
and that. And I was wearing it for luck.' He paused as if to
think about the luck, if luck it had been. 'That skull I buried
was a newish one. Don't ask me how I got my hands on it,
helped myself to it, you could say, and cleaned it up a bit.'
He did not mention how he had done this.

Stella, saying to herself, Talk, talk, it keeps the gun quiet,
asked him how he had known where to bury it.

'Oh, kids, I'm a local, we knew the place where they were.
A skull would turn up sometimes, and the dogs would have it,
or it would get kicked aside. One came up one day when were
larking about and the others wanted to use it as a football, but
I buried it.'

Another beginning for the obsession? Stella wondered what
the Neanderthals who buried the skulls first would have said.
Speechless, though, weren't they, give or take the odd grunt.
Pushed aside by a leaner, faster, articulate and more ruthless
race: *Homo sapiens*. She wondered if the races interbred and
produced a hybrid and if Sam was a descendant.

Then she looked into Sam's eyes and saw the clear ruthless
stare of *Homo sapiens*. No, he's one of us.

Behind her she thought she heard her husband trying to
use his mobile, so she raised her voice louder.

'So you went on killing?'

'The Walkers? They called themself the baby lovers, which
irritated me, but one of them, Lia, got to know what I was
doing . . . or I thought she did. Her husband was a good
guesser, and *knew* me. He'd been in the home with me and
he kicked the odd skull himself.'

He pointed his gun. 'So that's it, told you a lot, I wanted

210

to tell Joe, but he would never let me talk . . . Not that it'll do you lot any good.'

Here it comes, thought Stella.

'Happy Christmas,' said Sam.

Coffin pushed in front of Stella. Both of them would be between Marie and the gun. Paul flung himself on the bed, on top of Marie.

'Edge backwards, Stella,' Coffin whispered, freeing himself from Stella's grip to get at Sam before the gun went off.

Before him the door opened again. 'Watch it, Sam,' said Larry Lavender. 'You'll need a bullet for me.' He threw himself at Sam as the gun went off.

My turn now, thought Coffin, as he got one arm round Sam's body and another round his neck, wrenching him to the ground. 'Prison for you, my boy.'

'You could have been killed,' said Coffin to Larry Lavender, mopping at the blood on his chest and pressing on the wound to join it together.

'Not today,' said Larry gasping with pain. 'Not my death day.' He managed to grin. 'Be glad when the doctor gets here . . .'

'Here now,' said Coffin, stepping back.

'Could see him coming down the corridor. With a gun. Followed.'

'Glad you did. My good luck day.'

The doctor pushed Coffin aside. 'Here, let me get there. You'll kill this chap if you lean on his chest.'

'Not me,' Larry managed to get out.

'Let's hope so,' grunted the doctor, as he superintended Larry's departure for surgery. 'Now keep quiet, the less talking the better. Had any aspirin or garlic today?' Doctor, nurse and patient departed. Coffin watched them disappear into the lift.

'I hope he comes through,' he said to Stella. 'Let's get you home.'

She held back. 'I ought to say goodbye to Marie.'

211

'She's comfortably in her room, where we left her with her husband. Let's leave them together.'

They were driven home together in his official car. Coffin was thoughtful. Not one of my triumphs, he thought. I think Larry did better than me.

They had a quiet dinner together, with Stella admitting that it had been a tiring day. But she wanted to talk to her husband. There were things he must tell her.

'How did you know it was Sam?'

'Natasha told me.'

'What?'

'Forensics managed to bring up the letter she took with her.' Perhaps she had not meant in the end that he should read it. After all, she had taken it with her, not left it behind, but he had read it and grieved for her.

'It's a terrible story.'

'Tell me. What was it to do with Natasha?'

'She was guilty of murder. Of one murder at least, that of Mrs Jackson. She paid to have her killed.'

Stella stared at her husband. 'Why?'

The forensic experts had managed to bring up the text, almost complete, and had sent a copy that afternoon to Coffin.

'Hatred,' said Coffin sadly. 'And the others died because Sam found he enjoyed doing it. All connected with babies, you might notice. But the first one set him off. It was the first blow that counted.'

My baby was delivered by Mrs Jackson, born dead, she had said, *and she never let me even see. I didn't care how deformed it was, one head, two heads, no head, I wanted to see it. And perhaps it wasn't dead, but she let it die.*

'I think she was more than a little mad,' said Coffin sadly. Natasha had written out her pain in a careful print. *Wergild for my baby*, she had written, then scored it out. Almost out. She went on: *It festered inside when I saw my friends walking their babies, the way we had promised ourselves we would do. So I saved up all the money I could; I inserted a carefully worded advertisement in a free newspaper. If you read it more than once*

*you guessed what it meant. Sam answered and I paid him to do it.
I didn't know he would go on with the killing. All connected with
children or babies. My cousin guessed, I think. Or he thought she
did. For all those deaths I was guilty and could not live. I didn't
want to.*

'It's always hard to apportion guilt,' said Coffin, 'but yes, I
think she was right to accept guilt.'

'And her husband?'

'As well. I don't know what will happen to him. Folie à
deux, I think.'

As for Sam he did know, and Stella did not ask. He would
gladly have killed him if he had hurt Stella. Even in his
confession, if you could call it that, Sam had fudged the truth
here and there, put a gloss on it. The business of the ring,
for instance? He never told the truth there. Coffin felt there
would be a mystery to the end. Not all life tidies itself up.

Sam had admitted that he had seen Dr Murray studying
the skulls in the museum; he knew of her relationship with
his employer, Natasha, and thought she might be suspecting
him. As indeed perhaps she did. So he decided at once to
kill her, and he used the bucket of blood to throw suspicion
elsewhere. He wasn't quite clever enough to realize that in
the end it would all come back to him.

Coffin wanted to tell Stella that Marie had always been the
object of his gun at the christening, because she had once
worked in the obstetrics department and was associated with
births and babies in Sam's crazed mind. Not me, he wanted
to say, never me. He took a bus and set off to the killing. He
liked a bus ride, and he went on top to see out.

There was something he wanted her to see. He picked up
the folder containing the report that Paul Masters had made
for him; he had only just handed it in.

Coffin had a photograph in his hand. 'While on the job
Paul was snapped by a journalist with one of those cameras
that pop out the snap so you can see it straight away. Paul
grabbed it and took it away.' Didn't study it, though.

Coffin held it out to Stella.

There was Paul in the photograph, talking to one of the hospital staff.

'Nice-looking woman,' said Stella.

'One of the administrators . . . but it's not her. Look closer.'

In the background, in the shadows, there was another figure. Stella could just see the face. She looked up at her husband.

'Yes, it's Sam,' said Coffin, sadly. 'Got everywhere, didn't he?' He put the photograph away. 'If I had seen that earlier, the case might have ended there.' He did not blame Masters, only himself.

Stella said thoughtfully, 'Would make a good film. Might get my name in it.'

Coffin was quiet for a moment. Then he said, 'You might have a new name by then, Stella.'

She stared.

'Lady Coffin,' he said

'Well, well,' said Stella.

'I won't accept, if you don't want me to.'

Stella laughed. 'You don't mean that . . . but I do want it.' She mouthed her new name, 'Lady Coffin . . . I love it.'

In the morning, he went to see Larry Lavender.

'Thanks, Larry. You deserve a medal.' And Coffin would see he got one. 'How do you feel?'

'Not too bad at all. Just superficial, so the surgeon said.' He winced a bit as he drew breath. 'Mind you, I don't know what he calls superficial. Want a couple of vital organs punctured, I suppose.'

The pair looked at each other. There's a bond now, thought Coffin.

'That other business,' said Larry.

'Yes, I wondered about that.'

'Thought I didn't mind dying, eh? No, not my way. That was why I called that meeting . . . Go out with a bang, I thought. Anyway, it was a false alarm. A couple of doses of antibiotics for the wound, and Bob's your uncle. No alcohol, though, till the doses are over.'

'Good,' said Coffin.

He was still muttering, 'Good,' with general relief when he got into his office, thinking also to himself, 'My wife is one tough lady.'

There were were still points to puzzle over. But in any crime enquiry there were always unanswered questions, as Coffin knew well.

He worked away quietly until Paul Masters tapped on the door and came in.

'I thought you'd want to know at once, sir. A car has been found on the coast near St Andrews in Fife; a man and woman and dog inside. All dead. Gassed by the car fumes. I'm afraid it's the Lumsdens.'

Coffin went to the window to look out. It never ended, did it?